BEYOND THE SHADOWS

FOREBODING TALES OF TERROR

JAMES CIARDELLA

WARNING

Readers of this book BEWARE! You may think these are stories, but are they true? Tread with care, lest they happen to you. Ye be warned. Proceed at your own risk.

1

NEW SCHOOL

ASHLEY WAITED PATIENTLY BY THE FRONT door with her new book in hand. Of all the times for her mom to have overslept, she picked the worst possible day. It was Ashley's first day of third grade and being late to school was not ideal. To make matters worse, it was her first day at a new school, and she didn't know anyone. Ashley didn't know where to go and did not want to make a negative first impression.

"Are you ready, Mom?" Ashley asked hopefully up the stairs. There was no answer, so Ashley cracked open her book and began reading to pass the time.

Ashley's family moved to Sleepy Falls so her mom

could help take care of her ailing grandmother. Ashley didn't mind the move and was actually very excited to make new friends and live in the town where her mother had grown up. However, this was not her idea of a great first day. If only her father had taken her to school. He left for work at 6:30, which was far too early to be dropped off. Finally, Ashley's mom came downstairs.

"Okay, honey, let's hurry and get in the car," she said, as they dashed toward their grey Honda Civic. "I'm sorry I'm late, but I was up all night with your grandmother. She wasn't feeling very well last night."

"Okay, mom, can we hurry though? I don't even know where my classroom is."

"It is Room 39, sweetheart. They told me that it's on the third floor. Just follow the numbers, and you can't miss it."

The drive to school seemed to take forever. They passed house after house, street after street. This neighborhood was more beautiful than the one Ashley had lived in previously. The homes were modest sized, in excellent condition with freshly cut lawns and beautiful flowers in the front yard. Ashley gazed out her window admiring the houses and wondering if she would like her new school.

Finally, Ashley's mother pulled up in front of Hill Valley Elementary School. Ashley glanced at the car's clock. It read 9:15 – she was already 10 minutes late.

"Oh great," she thought to herself. "Just the way I

want to show up on the first day." Ashley quickly hopped out of the car and sprinted up the old stone steps to the main gate of the school. For being located in such a well-kept neighborhood, the school seemed out of place. The decrepit building looked like something out of a scary movie. The dark grey stone walls gave it an ominous look and Ashley had a feeling of foreboding as she entered the gate. The rusty hinges creaked open, and Ashley was inside the main hallway.

"All right, Mom said it's on the third floor. Here we go, I better hurry." Ashley sprinted up the stairs at top speed. She loved to run, and she was the fastest player on her previous soccer team. Ashley reached the second floor in a matter of seconds and began to take the stairs two at a time. Right before reaching the third floor, Ashley stubbed her foot on the side of one of the stairs and fell. Her knee bumped into the edge of the wood stair, and she knocked her head against the rail. Ashley laid on the stairs in a daze. "I'm not going to cry, not on my first day," she told herself. Ashley prided herself on her toughness.

"Are you okay, dear?" She looked up and saw an elderly woman at the top of the staircase. "You must have had a tremendous fall. I heard it all the way in my classroom."

"I'm okay," Ashley replied. The old lady smiled warmly at Ashley. Her eyes glimmered behind black glasses, and her grey hair was pulled up into a bun. She was short in stature, barely taller than Ashley. The woman carried a cane in one hand. She was wearing a full-length black and white dress.

"Well, dear, why don't you tell me your name, and where you're headed so I can help you out?"

"I'm Ashley, and I'm trying to find Room 39."

"Hee heh heh," she cackled. "Well, you are in luck today. I teach in Room 39 – it's my kingdom. I've been expecting you, Ashley. My name is Mrs. Yorp. Welcome to Hill Valley Elementary School." Ashley entered the classroom and looked around. An eerie, antique grand-father clock on the back wall drew her attention. Suddenly, she realized nineteen inquisitive faces had turned around to see the new girl joining the class.

"Class, this is Ashley. It is her first day at Hill Valley Elementary School. Who would like to show Ashley around today?" Immediately, 19 hands shot up to volunteer. "Okay, let's see… Lauren and Caitlin, you can do it. Ashley, why don't you go and sit down next to Lauren."

Ashley walked over to the empty desk, set her backpack down on the ground and plopped herself into the chair.

"Hi." Lauren smiled at her. She had her red hair pulled back into a pony-tail.

"Hello." Ashley grinned. Her dirty blonde hair hung a little past her shoulder, and she was a little taller than Lauren.

"Hi, Ashley. I'm Caitlin," the curly brunette next to

Lauren chimed in. "Where are you from?"

"I used to go to Reagan Elementary in Folsom. We just moved here," Ashley replied.

"Okay, listen up class." Mrs. Yorp interrupted Ashley getting to know her new friends. "Please do not touch the aquarium and tanks over in that corner of the classroom. Those are our class pets, and we will be using them to learn a little more about life science." The exotic fish in the aquarium caught Ashley's eyes initially, but then she shifted her gaze to the tanks. Two long snakes slithered inside the huge cage. "We have a few more items to go over." Mrs. Yorp reviewed the rest of the classroom rules.

"Does everyone understand?" The class nodded. "Excellent, now we are going to work on a math pre-test. Try your best, children. It will not be graded. I'm testing you to see how much you already know," Mrs. Yorp explained. Most of the questions were very easy for Ashley, and she flew through the test. At long last, it was recess.

"Come with me. I'll show you the school. We have the best playground." Lauren grabbed Ashley's hand and took off running for the jungle gym. Who needs a tour of the school when there are monkey bars to swing across, a cargo net to climb up, a suspension bridge to run across, and three mountainous slides to slide down? The three girls yelped with excitement as they scurried all over the play structure. A few minutes later, the bell rang, interrupting Ashley's fun. Hurriedly, Ashley, Caitlin, and Lauren ran to get in line.

"Just wait until lunch – we have way longer to play!" Caitlin exclaimed. Ashley loved Hill Valley Elementary already. The girls continued talking in line until Mrs. Yorp hobbled out of her classroom and around the corner to where her class waited.

"All right children," she gurgled. "As soon as we are quiet we can go inside. We have lots to learn today." Mrs. Yorp glared at the students until they were quiet. It only took a few seconds – this was the first day after all. Room 39 marched back to class in single file. The students took their seats, and Mrs. Yorp had planned an art project for the students for the remainder of the morning. Ashley listened as Mrs. Yorp showed them an example of what she expected. She had crafted an art project of a campfire. It was an impressive 3D project inside a shoebox. Enormous flames appeared to be leaping out of the shoebox. Several people were seated around the campfire. Mrs. Yorp explained that this is what had been her most memorable experience of the previous summer.

"My favorite part of summer was sitting around the campfire telling stories. I just LOVE campfires." Ashley could not picture Mrs. Yorp camping. "I want everyone to depict their favorite summer activity. It can be a drawing, a painting, or a 3D picture. I have crayons, markers, paint, and other supplies up here. I will excuse you by your table."

Ashley decided she would make a 3D picture of her friend Natalie's swimming pool. She had spent practically the whole summer swimming. Like most 9-year-old children, it was her favorite thing to do.

Ashley was nearly finished with her 3D project when Mrs. Yorp shuffled by with her cane.

"You like the water, eh?" she smirked.

Ashley looked up and nodded. "I love swimming." Mrs. Yorp turned away and mumbled something as she limped toward another child's desk. Ashley couldn't hear what she said.

"She must not like my picture," Ashley thought. "What is wrong with it?" Ashley had created one of the best pictures of her young life. "This is going to be a difficult year if Mrs. Yorp is that tough to please."

Eventually, everyone finished their art projects, and it was time for lunch. Ashley stood in line to buy lunch because her mom hadn't packed one this morning. Ashley hated corndogs, so naturally, the cafeteria served corndogs today. She had a bad experience with them when she was 7. To make matters worse, she received a scorched corndog. It was almost entirely black as if it had been left in a fire too long. Ashley didn't even bother asking for a new one. Burned or not, she wasn't going to eat that garbage on a stick.

Ashley wolfed down her fruit cup, french fries, and milk in record time. She wanted as much time as possible to play on the playground. The girls enjoyed a raucous game of tag all over the jungle gym. Lunchtime flew by, and so did the rest of the day. Before Ashley knew it, it was time for her to go home.

"Bye Lauren. Bye Caitlin, see you tomorrow!" Ashley yelled as she ran from her classroom. She floated all the way to her house. Ashley loved her new school, despite her mixed feelings about Mrs. Yorp. Sometimes she seemed nice, but sometimes Mrs. Yorp was a little strange. "Oh well, I already made great friends in Lauren and Caitlin," she thought. At night, Ashley told her mom and dad all about Caitlin, Lauren, and the fantastic playground.

"It's great that you love your new school, champ!" Ashley's father told her. "I knew you would make friends quickly."

Ashley had trouble falling asleep because she was so excited and couldn't wait to go back to school tomorrow. She drifted off to sleep an hour later still replaying the day's thrills in her mind.

It seemed like only a moment later the bright sun shining through her window shook her from dreamland. Ashley sprung out of bed, threw on her clothes and raced downstairs to fix herself breakfast.

"Mom, are you ready? I don't want to be late to school today," Ashley called out between mouthfuls of Cheerios.

"I'm almost ready honey. You won't be late."

For once, her mother was right. Ashley didn't just get to school on time. She arrived 10 minutes early. "Even better," thought Ashley. "I have more time to play with my friends." Ashley began looking around for Lauren and Caitlin. They didn't seem to be anywhere.

"Oh well," she thought. "I'm sure they will be here soon." Finally, the bell rang to go to class, and still, Ashley didn't see Caitlin, Lauren or any of her friends from yesterday.

"They must be waiting at the classroom." Ashley realized as she made her way up the stairs to Room 39. Upon reaching the third floor, Ashley was baffled. Lining up in front of Room 39 were 19 new students and a new teacher.

"What happened to my class? Where did they go?" The thoughts raced through Ashley's head. She began to look around to see if Mrs. Yorp and her class were going into a different room today.

"Good morning, I see a new face back there. You must be Ashley," the strange lady smiled at her. "We missed you yesterday."

"Umm…where is Mrs. Yorp's class?" Ashley was confused.

"Who's class?" The teacher now had a confused look on her face to match Ashley's.

"The teacher I was with yesterday, Mrs. Yorp, and

where are Lauren and Caitlin? What is going on?"

"Ashley, there is no Mrs. Yorp at this school. My name is Mrs. Silver, and you are going to be in my class this year.

"Wait, I don't understand. Yesterday I was in Mrs. Yorp's class with Lauren and Caitlin. What happened to them?" The other children in line were giving Ashley funny looks, but she was too disconcerted to notice.

"Ashley, you were absent yesterday. Did you go to a different school by mistake?"

"No, no, no. I was here yesterday. I remember the big grey front gate, and the monkey bars and the cargo net. I was here!" Ashley was almost beside herself with frustration. "Where is my class?!"

"Ok, children, go in, sit down, and get your books out. I'll be inside in a minute. Ashley, we'll get this figured out." Mrs. Silver smiled sweetly and seemed to be genuinely concerned. "I'm going to call down to the office, and you can go talk to the principal. Maybe he can get to the bottom of this."

"Okay," Ashley sighed reluctantly. She felt like she was in a bad dream.

Mrs. Silver walked into the classroom. Ashley could see the antique grandfather clock on the back wall again. This was the exact same classroom. She stepped inside but stayed by the door. Ashley knew something wasn't right, and she wanted to stay close to her only escape hatch. She was still in a daze thinking about what had transpired when she heard a voice calling her name.

"Ashley, this is Paula. She will walk you down to the office." A worried look replaced Mrs. Silver's smile. Ashley felt even less at ease, but she followed Paula out the door without a word. The two girls walked down the two flights of stairs, through the hall, and to the office.

Paula broke the silence as they reached the office door. "Don't worry, Mr. Kimmerly is cool. Bye."

"Thank you," Ashley mumbled as she turned the handle to the large grey door. Inside two middle-aged women peered at their computers, obviously very busy.

"Umm… excuse me; I'm here to see the principal." Ashley was still trying to figure out what was going on. The short, brown-haired secretary on the right glanced up from behind thick glasses.

"You can go in, honey, Mr. Kimmerly's office is right there," she swiveled halfway around in her chair and pointed at a room toward the back of the office. Head down, Ashley walked around the lady's work station to Mr. Kimmerly's office.

"Come on in, you must be Ashley." Mr. Kimmerly was a kind looking man who appeared to be in his early 40s. Beneath his well-groomed mustache was a smile that welcomed Ashley into the tidy office. "Why don't you have a seat and tell me what seems to be the trouble." Mr. Kimmerly eased into his leather chair.

"Well, sir, I can't find my class. I went back to the same room I was in yesterday, and there is a new class with a new teacher and new students." Ashley studied Mr. Kimmerly's face to see if he had any answers.

"Okay, Ashley, what room were you in yesterday?"

"Room 39, the same one I went to this morning."

"Are you sure?"

"Yes. Mrs. Yorp was there, and Lauren and Ca-"

"Who was your teacher?" Mr. Kimmerly's smile had disappeared. His eyebrows furrowed and a look of concern took over his face. It troubled Ashley. "What was wrong?" she wondered.

"Mrs. Yorp. Why?" Ashley asked him.

"Ashley, here is the problem. Mrs. Silver has taught in Room 39 for the last four years, including yesterday. Nobody by the name of Mrs. Yorp works here. You were absent yesterday. Are you sure you didn't go to a different school by mistake? Sometimes these things happen." Ashley was more perplexed than ever. She knew she went to this school yesterday. She recognized the playground and Room 39. Everything looked exactly the same, except all the people were different.

"No sir, I'm sure I was here yesterday."

"Okay. Here's what we are going to do. I am going to give your mother a call, and maybe she can come down here so we can sort all this out." Mr. Kimmerly picked up the phone as he scrolled through the student directory until he reached M. "McCall, ah here it is." He quickly dialed the number. Ashley could hear the phone ringing. Finally, after what seemed like forever, it went to voicemail.

"Hello, you have reached Susan McCall. I'm not available right now. Please leave a message, and I will call you back. Thank you. Beeeeeep"

"Hello, Mrs. McCall. This is Mr. Kimmerly, the principal at Hill Valley Elementary school. I would like to ask you a couple of questions. If you could give me a call at your earliest convenience, I would appreciate it very much. Thank you." Mr. Kimmerly appeared disappointed.

"Okay, Ashley, does your mom have a work number?"

"No. My mom doesn't work."

"Do you know your father's work number?"

"No, sir, he just started a new job." Mr. Kimmerly was running out of ideas.

"Tell you what; I will continue to try to contact your mother. Meanwhile, why don't you get to know your new class? Mrs. Silver is a fantastic teacher, and I'm sure you will enjoy her."

"All right," Ashley sighed.

"I will call you down to the office as soon as I get a hold of your mom."

Ashley stood up and slowly trudged out of the office. She wandered back to Room 39 in a stupor. Ashley couldn't make sense of her meeting with Mr. Kimmerly.

She could not have dreamed up yesterday. Her imagination was not that good.

"Maybe I can find Caitlin and Lauren at recess. They'll help me figure out what is going on." With this comforting thought, Ashley entered the classroom and prepared for another first day. Ashley had difficulty focusing on her school work. Most of the time she had no idea what Mrs. Silver was saying. She was too busy thinking about recess, and whether Mr. Kimmerly would be able to contact her mom.

"Janice, I haven't been able to reach Susan McCall. Would you please continue to call her every so often?"

"Of course, John."

"Did you hear what Ashley said?" Mr. Kimmerly asked Janice.

"No. What?"

"She claimed she was in Mrs. Yorp's classroom yesterday. Where do you think she got that name from?"

"She must have talked to someone from the town. Why would she even joke about that?" Janice was now quite irritated.

"You think she made up the story to cause trouble?"

"Of course I do. Ashley talked to someone in the town and thought it would be funny to do this on her first day of school. That girl is trouble, John."

"She didn't seem like she was lying. We need to get Mrs. McCall on the phone. That should shed some light on this situation." Mr. Kimmerly turned and walked out of the office.

At recess, Ashley roamed around searching for Lauren and Caitlin. She could not believe that her friends had just vanished. Several girls from her new class tried to ask Ashley to play with them.

"I'm sorry. I don't feel well," was all Ashley could think to say. She didn't want them to believe the new kid was crazier than they already thought. Finally, the bell rang. It was time to go in from recess, and there was still no sign of Lauren or Caitlin. With a heavy sigh, Ashley made her way to line up for class.

The rest of the school day was a blur to Ashley. She couldn't concentrate on anything. Yesterday kept replaying in her head.

"Was it a dream?" she thought to herself. At lunchtime, Mr. Kimmerly updated her. They still had not been able to reach her mother. Now, Ashley began to worry about her mom.

When the school day finally ended, Ashley raced home as quickly as her two legs would carry her. She didn't want to be at this crazy school a second longer. Ashley's house was two miles away. By the time she reached the end of the street, she was out of breath and slowed her pace to a quick walk. As she rounded the corner and turned left onto Bettencourt Drive, she started to smell smoke. Ashley looked up.

"What is happening?" she thought. At the end of the street were two fire trucks, an ambulance, and thick smoke plumes. Ashley sprinted down the road. Her house sat at the end of this street.

"Mom! Mom!!! Mom!" she started screaming as she scrambled closer. When she was within 30 feet of the fire trucks, she could see her house was the one on fire.

"Mom!" A fireman intercepted her before she could advance any closer to the blaze.

"Easy, honey. You can't go in there. Do you live here?" The fireman tried to get her attention, but Ashley couldn't hear him because she was screaming and crying.

"Ashley! Are you ok?" A familiar voice called from behind her. Ashley whirled around to see her mother jumping out of her car. She darted up to Ashley, and they embraced.

"I –I thought you …"

"I know, honey. I'm fine. I'm right here." Ashley's mom comforted Ashley.

"Where were you?"

"I was taking care of Grandma. I was at her house all day. She asked me to come over because she wasn't feeling well. I guess it's a good thing I went," she whispered ruefully.

Ashley and her mom watched the firefighters extinguish the blaze for an hour. Finally, one of them came up to Ashley's mom.

"Mrs. McCall, we've put out the fire. It appears it

originated in the living room. We're not sure what caused it – possibly a lamp left on. Would you like us to do anything for you?" The firefighter smiled sympathetically.

"No thank you. We're just going to look around for anything we can salvage and then we will stay at my mom's tonight. Thank you for everything you did. Please thank all the firefighters for us."

"You're welcome, ma'am. Good luck to you." He turned and strode back to the fire truck.

Ashley and her mother warily walked toward the rubble that used to be their house. Much of the exterior was still intact, but inside was a different story. There were ashes everywhere, and Ashley hardly recognized the place. The living room was a disaster and contained nothing salvageable. Ashley followed her mom down the hall toward the family room.

"What the..." Ashley's mom couldn't finish her sentence. The family room was utterly charred except for a little 3-foot square in the dead center of the room. Amidst all the ashes sat a perfectly undisturbed piece of carpet. On the floor laid something that caught Ashley's eye. She crunched through the ashes and bent down to pick up the object that had grabbed her attention. It was a photograph. A look of bewilderment spread over Ashley's face as she examined the photo.

"What's wrong, honey?" her mom's curiosity was piqued.

Ashley continued to stare at the picture.

"Let me see, sweetheart." Ashley handed the picture to her mother. Now it was Ashley's mom's turn to look baffled.

"What in the world is this doing here?" Mrs. McCall whispered.

"Do you know her?" Ashley questioned her mother.

"Huh…um…yea," Mrs. McCall seemed stupefied. "This is the woman that almost killed me a long time ago. I was in third grade, and I hated it. I had the meanest teacher in the world. I used to fake stomachaches to get out of her class. One day at lunch, I pulled my usual stunt, pretending to be sick. The secretary kept trying to talk me into going back. All of a sudden the fire alarm went off. I remember leaving the office thinking it was a drill. When I got outside, I saw smoke coming from my classroom. People were screaming. My teacher had gone crazy, lit the classroom on fire and locked the children inside. Nobody survived. She killed herself and all my friends, Caitlin and Lauren…all of them. The only reason I'm still alive is that I faked…"

"Who did you say your friends were Mom?" Ashley interrupted.

"Caitlin and Lauren – they were the best." Mrs. Mc-Call had a sad smile on her face now.

"Can I see that photograph again?" Ashley's mom handed it back to her daughter. Ashley gazed at the picture in disbelief. Leering back at her with a sinister grin was Mrs. Yorp.

2

THE SHORTSTOP

LUKE WAGGLED HIS BAT IN THE RIGHT SIDE of the batter's box and glared at the pitcher. His shaggy brown hair crawled out beneath his helmet. The lanky boy on the mound rocked into his wind-up and fired the ball. Luke's hands exploded forward, and he heard the sweet sound of bat meeting ball. The tall, athletic batter sprinted out of the box as his blast screamed toward right-center field. Luke accelerated into top gear and cruised into third base standing up for his second hit of the day.

Luke's triple led off the fourth inning, but the Yankees were unable to drive him in to break the 3-3 tie. Luke shook his head in disgust as he walked back to the dugout.

"Nice hit, Luke. Now go shut 'em down," said Coach Tom. Pitching was Luke's favorite part of baseball and he took the mound for his first inning of the day. The Royals' shortstop, Donnie, strode to the plate.

Luke rocked and fired. "PING!" The sound of aluminum bat meeting ball surprised him. Donnie had cued a groundball toward the Yankees' second baseman, Bryan. At the last moment, the ball spun right and ticked off his glove into right field.

"Come on!" Luke glared at Bryan. Luke's focus remained on the error and he walked Andrew and Ty on eight straight pitches. Now he was irritated with himself.

"Time!" Coach Tom asked the umpire for a mound visit. "Settle down, Luke. Just throw strikes, and we'll get these guys out. Let's go!"

The pep talk calmed Luke down and he struck out the next two hitters with ease. Luke spun a curveball to Tim, the Royals' cleanup hitter. He lofted a fly ball to right field. Devin wobbled under the pop-up, but the ball glanced off the raven-haired boy's glove. All three runners scored on the play, and Tim chugged into second base.

"WHAT ARE YOU DOING?!" Luke screamed as he spiked his glove into the ground. Joey singled up the middle to make it 7-3 before Luke struck out another batter to finally put the nightmare inning behind him.

In the dugout, his manager tried to calm him down.

"Luke, you can't get upset out there. You and your team-mates play worse when you're angry. They're afraid to make a mistake. Encourage them, don't scream at them."

"Whatever," Luke muttered. Baseball defined Luke and was the most precious thing in his life. He couldn't tolerate failure. His teammates all stood on the other side of the dugout to avoid his ire. Coach Tom shook his head and walked away.

In the top of the sixth, the Yankees rallied for three runs to make the score 7-6. Sergio and Devin were on second and third base with two outs and Luke at the plate.

"Time to win this game," thought Luke. He oozed confidence. Juan, the Royals' pitcher, threw a curveball on the first pitch. "PING!" A shot down the left-field line!

"FOUL!" The ball had landed a foot outside the line. Luke worked the count to three balls and one strike, before Juan rocked back and fired one over the middle of the plate.

"PING!" Luke slammed his bat down in frustration. He watched helplessly as Tim glided over to medium left-center and squeezed the routine fly ball for the final out. Luke threw his helmet against the fence. His team-mates ignored his embarrassing display. Luke sulked in the dugout and refused to shake hands with the Royals.

Coach Tom pulled Luke aside after the game. "You

know, Luke, when I played baseball, I would lose my temper, get upset with my teammates, and get down on myself when we lost." Luke stared at the ground wishing he could disappear.

"No one enjoyed being around me. In college, I had a teammate who changed all of that. He was the most positive person I have ever met. He encouraged everyone on our team. He was extremely humble even though he was the best player. It made me a better person. I started patterning my behavior after him. The man I'm talking about was your father." Luke looked up in surprise. "I know you can be a leader, too, Luke."

"I'm sorry, coach. I'll try to be better," Luke said half-heartedly. "My mom never told me about my dad. I wish I could have met him."

"He was a great man, son, and you can be, too." Coach Tom patted him on the shoulder. Luke started the long trek home, replaying the painful loss in his head.

After walking for 15 minutes, Luke reached his green and yellow one-story house. The front yard was un-kempt and taken over by weeds. The lawn was brown in some spots and knee-high in other places. The over-grown hedges needed trimming, and several plants were dead. The paint on the outside of the house had faded, and Luke hated the colors. He climbed up his steps and pulled open the screen door. Luke sighed, turned the knob, and pushed open the front door.

Inside, the house was dark, even though it was the middle of the day. As usual, Luke's mom had drawn all the curtains and slept curled up on the couch. Just once he wished she would come to his game. She'd never seen Luke play and never asked about the game. Sometimes Luke wondered if she even knew he was on a team.

Luke ventured into the kitchen to get something to eat. In the sink, a pile of dirty dishes greeted him. As quietly as he could, Luke began cleaning the mess. He didn't want to wake up his mother. She seemed to sleep longer these days. Luke figured she must be exhausted. After he finished tidying up the kitchen, Luke made himself a sandwich for lunch. His favorite was peanut butter and jelly, but they were out of jam, so a peanut butter sandwich would have to do. He noticed a new book on the kitchen table. He loved reading while he was eating, so he cracked open the book to check it out.

"Luke, are you home?" Luke's mom stirred.

"Yeah, I'm here."

"Are you hungry, dear?"

"I got a sandwich, thanks," Luke replied.

"Okay," she mumbled before popping on the television. Luke spent the rest of the afternoon wondering what it would be like to have a mom who cared about what he was doing.

At Monday's practice, Coach Tom had the Yankees work on fielding for half an hour before dividing into four groups for batting practice. As Luke was digging into the batter's box, he noticed a boy walking in from center field. Luke didn't recognize him, so he stepped out. Coach Tom turned around, following Luke's gaze. The whole practice halted as this bushy-haired person approached the Yankees' coach. He was about Luke's height and build with brown hair, and he carried a bat and glove.

"Hi, I'm Richie. I just got to town, and I was wondering if I could practice with you guys." The kid sported a goofy smile.

"Sure, Richie. I'm Coach Tom. Why don't you jump into Luke's group? That's Luke, Tommy, and Sergio." Coach Tom pointed to each player.

"What's up?" they nodded at Richie.

What's up, guys."

Luke jumped in the box and began ripping line drives all over the field. He stepped out satisfied. After Sergio and Tommy hit, Richie stepped to the plate. Luke watched him intently. He held his hands shoulder high and moved the bat in a slow circle. It looked like a mirror image of Luke's batting style. On the first pitch, Richie pulled a majestic drive to deep right-center field. The ball cleared the fence by 50 feet. Coach Tom's jaw dropped. He repeated the feat with the next two pitches, and the whole team stared in awe at the new player.

"Nice hitting, Richie!" Tommy and Sergio were quite impressed.

"Thanks. You guys hit well, too." Richie replied with a sheepish grin.

Luke stared silently at Richie. He despised anyone upstaging him. Richie's presence caused everyone to play better. The Yankees began to look like a good baseball team.

"Great catch, Luke!" Richie encouraged somebody on every play.

Coach Tom spoke to the team at the end of practice. "Great job, everyone. Best we've looked all season. Richie, are you interested in playing for the Yankees?"

A huge smile spread across Richie's olive-skinned face. "That would be great!"

"Excellent. I'll get you a uniform for Thursday. Welcome to the Yankees."

"Okay, he did pretty well in practice, but we'll see how he does in a real game," thought Luke. "Anyone can look good in practice."

The days between games always felt like an eternity to Luke. This week was no different, but game day eventually arrived. Today, the fourth-place Yankees were playing the first-place Orioles. Luke felt winning this game was imperative.

Luke took the mound, and Coach Tom inserted the new player, Richie, at shortstop. Luke struck out all three batters to begin the game. The Yankees scored five runs in the first three innings. Luke and Richie had two doubles apiece.

"He's not even cocky," thought Luke. Richie had complimented everyone, just like at practice. By now, Luke was happy to have him on the team.

They led 5-0 entering the fifth inning. Luke was cruising and hadn't allowed a hit yet. Michael, the Orioles' leadoff batter hit a sharp grounder to third base. Jeff misplayed the bounce for an error.

"Aw man! What are you doing?" thought Luke, trying to hide his anger.

"Don't worry about that, Jeff. Shake it off! Way to keep it in front of you." Luke whirled around to see Richie giving Jeff a pep talk. Jeff seemed to perk up. However, Luke began to tire. With two outs, he gave up consecutive hits to load the bases.

"Time!" Coach Tom jogged out of the dugout. "Great game, Luke! We're going to bring in Bryan. Richie, move over to second, Luke you're at short."

Luke moped while departing the mound. Richie met him at shortstop.

"Way to pitch." Luke glanced up to see Richie's smiling face.

"Thanks," mumbled Luke. "They shouldn't have gotten any hits off me. That last ball was a strike. Stupid umpire…" Luke could feel the frustration welling up inside.

"Hey, shake it off man. You did great. Just focus on the next play."

Luke shook his head. "Richie's crazy. How can I be happy? I just got pulled."

"CRACK!" The sound of bat meeting ball woke Luke up from his thoughts. David's blast was screaming in his direction. He got his glove down a fraction of a second late, and the ball caromed off his glove toward second base. Luke scrambled after it in a desperate attempt to recover. As he sprinted to the bag, he saw Richie snatch the ball out of the air and step on second base to get the force out and end the inning.

Again, Luke hung his head as he trotted off the field. Richie noticed Luke sulking in the dugout. "Way to stay in front of that rocket, man. You saved a couple of runs."

"Nah, you saved me. I booted it," Luke muttered as he bumped fists with Richie.

"Keep your head up and stop being so hard on yourself. LET'S GO, SERGIO!" Richie encouraged his teammates until the final out of the Yankees' 7-3 win.

The next day at school, Luke sat in class daydreaming about the game. "I should have caught that ball." Luke couldn't let it go.

"How about you, Luke? What did you answer?" Mrs. Kettlebaum called on him interrupting his thoughts.

"Stupid Mrs. Kettlebaum. She's always picking on me," Luke thought as he looked at the board and glanced at his neighbor's paper.

"The answer is NOT on Ann's paper, Luke. Are you

paying attention? Of course, you're not."

"It's hard to pay attention when you are so boring." Luke regretted the words as soon as they came out of his mouth, but he hated being mocked in front of the class.

"What did you say?" snapped Mrs. Kettlebaum. She rumbled over to his desk.

Luke lowered his eyes and tried not to look at the confrontational Mrs. Kettlebaum. He didn't want to get in trouble again, but he didn't know what to say.

"I'm waiting, Luke." He sank lower in the seat and kept his chin on his chest.

"I'm tired of this, Luke. You can't just shut down during class. If you don't want to answer me, then you can go down to the office and explain it to Mrs. Bryant."

"Great," thought Luke. "I have to go see the principal again. That's the third time this week – she's going to call home." He tried to ignore Mrs. Kettlebaum and sit silently.

She wasn't going to fall for it. "Luke, you need to go right now or I will have Mrs. Bryant come get you."

Luke had no choice but to admit defeat. With a huge sigh, he lifted himself out of his chair and sullenly trudged to the office.

"Oh well, going to the office is better than listening to Mrs. Kettlebaum blabber on and on," he told himself as he walked the familiar path. Luke snuck into the office and sat in his usual chair. The secretaries rolled their eyes.

"Welcome back, Luke. What did you do now?" Ms.

Debbi asked him. Luke did not reply.

"We're going to put your name on that chair – you're here so much," Ms. Patti chuckled.

Now it was Luke's turn to roll his eyes. Patiently he waited for the principal to see him. Mrs. Bryant rarely came down hard on Luke. She realized Mrs. Kettlebaum tended to overreact. Luke speculated that she felt sorry for him, but he knew she would eventually run out of patience. Mrs. Bryant would be just like every other adult he had ever met. She would let him down.

After a couple of minutes, Mrs. Bryant appeared at the door to her office with a look of disappointment on her face. He expected to get yelled at this time.

"Okay, Luke. Why are you here?"

"Mrs. Kettlebaum told me to come here."

"Well, yeah," Mrs. Bryant laughed a little. "I figured that out. What did you do that got you sent to see me?"

"I don't know. I didn't do anything. I just didn't know an answer, and then Mrs. Kettlebaum yelled at me for not paying attention."

"Were you paying attention?"

"No."

"Okay, did anything else happen?"

"I said she was boring."

"Why did you say that, Luke?"

"Because SHE IS."

Mrs. Bryant tried to hide a smile. "Even if you think

she is boring, is it okay to say that in the middle of class?"

Luke looked down. "No," he muttered.

"You know you need to pay attention in class. We've talked about this before. If your grades are bad this quarter, you are going to have tutoring after school."

Luke nodded.

"It's five minutes until lunch. You can stay here now, but after lunch I want you to apologize to Mrs. Kettlebaum. Otherwise, there will be further consequences."

Luke nodded again.

"Okay, you can go wait out in the main office."

When the bell rang, Luke exited the office and began walking to the cafeteria.

"Hey, Luke!" a familiar voice called out. Luke glanced to his left and was shocked to see Richie.

"Richie, I didn't know you went to school here." Luke hoped Richie hadn't seen him come from the office.

"I just started this week. Are you going to lunch?"

"Yeah."

"Sweet, let's go."

Luke gave Richie a scouting report on the A's while they ate. Usually Luke didn't have anyone to talk to at lunch. Most of his classmates were intimidated by his attitude and didn't want to be around him. It frustrated Luke, but he didn't know what to do.

"Hey, Richie, do you want to come over to my house tomorrow after our game?"

"Yeah, that'd be great," Richie replied exuberantly.

"Do you like whiffle ball? We can play in my front yard."

"Whiffle ball is awesome. I got a nasty splitter though."

Luke was looking forward to whiffle ball so much that he almost forgot to apologize to Mrs. Kettlebaum. Fortunately, Mrs. Bryant was there standing next to the classroom. Her sideways glance reminded Luke of his obligation.

"I'm sorry for not paying attention and calling you boring, Mrs. Kettlebaum," Luke said in the most apologetic voice he could muster.

"Okay, Luke. Thank you. Try to listen during class. I want you to do well." Luke didn't believe her, but he managed to stay out of trouble for the rest of the day. He even paid attention a little bit, although he didn't complete any of his class work.

The next day the Yankees locked horns with the last-place A's. Luke got off to a great start by hitting a two-run home run in the first inning. In the third inning, he singled, and Richie hit a triple to make it 3-0. Johnny gave up a two-run home run to Clint in the bottom of the fourth inning, allowing the A's to close the gap. Luke blasted a double in the fifth as the Yankees exploded for seven runs.

In the top of the sixth, Luke came up again looking

for his fourth hit of the game. On the two-balls, two-strikes pitch, Luke took a mighty cut but missed for strike three.

Luke moped back to the dugout. When he reached the bat rack, he dropped his bat and helmet with disdain. Luke sought out the empty back corner and slumped on the bench. Richie detected Luke's poor body language. "Shake it off, Luke."

The Yankees won 11-3, but Luke's last at-bat sapped the joy from him. After reviewing the ill-fated swing for 10 minutes, Luke finally realized he did have three hits. "I guess I did okay." Luke's mood improved when he realized Richie was coming over. He went to the garage to get the whiffle ball and bat. They were covered in cobwebs. Apparently, he hadn't played in a while. Luke stepped outside just as Richie arrived.

"Hey, Luke!"

"What's up, Richie?" Luke replied. He was excited to have a friend over for once.

"You played great today, Luke. I can't wait until our next game."

"Yeah, I can't wait either. Do you want to play some whiffle ball?"

"All right, let's go."

"Past me is a single, the sidewalk is a double, and on the grass is a home run."

"Sounds good, that's how I usually play."

"So, he's played before," thought Luke. He couldn't let Richie beat him.

Neither boy could muster a hit through three innings. In the top of the final frame, Richie blasted a double. He tattooed the next pitch onto the grass to make it 2-0. Luke's smile disappeared and was replaced with frustration.

After he struck out to begin the final inning, he exploded. "STOP CHEATING!" Luke slammed the bat on the concrete. He was embarrassed, but couldn't stop himself. Luke continued to pound the driveway while Richie just stared silently at his antics.

"Pitch the ball!" Luke snapped. Richie threw the ball. Luke took a mighty swing that produced a slow groundball. As Richie got down to field it for the final out, the ball hit a rock and shot over his shoulder. Richie grinned as he chased Luke's first hit. Luke blooped the next pitch into the middle of the street. Richie sprinted backward and stretched his hands out in an attempt to snag the pop-up. To Luke's relief, the ball landed just out of Richie's reach. Luke expected to see some frustration on Richie's face, but he grabbed the ball and jogged back to the pitcher's mound with a smile on his face.

"Nice hit."

Richie's next toss did not break as much as usual. "WHACK!" Luke looked up and saw the ball land in the middle of the grass. Richie had a sheepish grin plastered on his face. "Nice game, Luke. You got to give me a rematch next week."

Luke stood there foolishly. He didn't feel like he had just won. In fact, Luke was ashamed of his behavior. He wished he hadn't hit that home run.

"Uh… sure. Look, I'm sorry for losing my temper." Luke couldn't even look Richie in the eye.

"Hey, no problem, thanks for inviting me over to play whiffle ball."

"Yeah, you're welcome. How come you don't lose your temper? I got so lucky to win that game, and all you did was congratulate me, even after everything I did."

"I enjoy competing, and that game was exciting. I know we're both good players. I can't win every time, but I love playing. Why do you get so upset?"

Richie caught Luke off guard. He had never really thought about it before. "Um… I think when I lose, I doubt my ability. I feel like everyone is looking at me and thinking I'm terrible."

"I see what you mean," Richie replied. "You need to stay confident. As good as you are, one failure shouldn't change the way you see yourself. My dad told me that everyone fails, but the way you deal with failure determines whether you are a success or not. I always try to remember that."

"Your dad gave you good advice. My dad didn't teach me anything. I don't even remember him. He died fighting a fire when I was 2." Luke didn't know why he was telling Richie this. He had never talked to anyone about his dad before.

"I'm sorry. That's terrible. You know, my mom told me once that our relatives watch over us from Heaven. I know your dad is looking down, and he's proud of you."

Luke hadn't considered Heaven before. It comforted him to believe he had someone watching over him who cared.

"It's cool to think he could actually see me play. Sometimes I wish he could be at my games. I would love to play catch with him just once," Luke opened up. "One time I dreamt that we played baseball together. It was awesome." Luke smiled at the memory.

"Yeah, I bet that would be great," Richie agreed. The boys hung out for the rest of the day. Luke didn't realize how much he missed having friends.

The next week at school was Luke's best since kindergarten. He kept Richie's dad's advice in his head and endeavored to control his attitude. Luke completed all of his class work and homework. He focused in class, and treated Mrs. Kettlebaum with respect… most of the time. This change in Luke coincided with a continued hot streak for the Yankees. They went 12-2 to finish the season 15-5 overall and in second place.

The only team they couldn't defeat in the second half was the first-place Orioles. Luke controlled his emotions much better, except for the two losses to them. He threw his helmet in frustration after having his worst games of the year. "Shake it off, Luke. Remember…it's not whether you succeed or fail, but how you react," Richie reminded him. The Yankees would have to defeat the Orioles twice in the playoffs to win the championship.

In school, Luke maintained his trend toward becoming a decent student. Most of his grades were now B's, and his behavior had significantly improved. Mrs. Kettlebaum severely tested Luke's newfound attitude on the Friday before the big playoff game. The class had a math test the day before, and Luke nervously waited for the results. Recently, Luke had performed better in math, but he wasn't entirely confident with it yet. Finally, Mrs. Kettlebaum shuffled over to his desk and dropped his test with a smirk on her face.

Slowly, Luke turned over the paper and peered at the top right corner; 67 percent. The score crushed Luke's spirit. He put his head down and started to sulk. Mrs. Kettlebaum began to review the test, and Luke mustered the will to glance up and listen. He realized two of his answers were mistakenly marked incorrect. Near the end of the test, Luke noticed two more answers erroneously crossed out.

"I'm going to get a B after all," Luke thought to himself, after adding up the extra points he was sure to get. When Mrs. Kettlebaum finished, Luke approached her desk.

"Um… Mrs. Kettlebaum, I think I got these problems correct," he stammered as he showed her the four problems.

Mrs. Kettlebaum skeptically peered through her glasses at Luke's paper. "Luke, what are you trying to pull here?" Her shrill, high-pitched voice always scared Luke. "I see eraser marks on this paper. Did you erase your answers and write in the correct ones while we were going over the test?"

"No, I didn't" was all Luke could think to say.

"If you can't be honest with me, then you can go see Mrs. Bryant."

Luke felt the rage bubble up inside of him. Mrs. Kettlebaum was utterly unfair. Luke was tempted to yell at Mrs. Kettlebaum, call her names, and rip up his test. Right before he lost control, Richie's advice popped into his head, "The only thing you can control is how you react."

Luke bit his tongue, quietly turned around and marched out of the classroom. As upset as Luke was, he also was strangely proud of himself.

Mrs. Bryant went easy on Luke, as usual. "Why don't you hang out here for a little bit and then go back to class? I will talk to Mrs. Kettlebaum after school."

Luke's furor subsided after cooling down in the office. Mrs. Kettlebaum spoke to him five minutes before the end of school.

"Okay, I am going to change your grade on the test. Next time, you need to raise your hand and let me know while we are going over the test. Do you understand?"

Luke nodded his head. He was amazed. Richie's dad's philosophy really worked. Luke had never been more excited at school. He almost forgot about the playoff game.

Saturday morning arrived, and Luke woke up bright and early. He had never been in a championship game before, and the Yankees had only one win against the Orioles all year. Today was going to be the day. Luke could feel it when he arrived at the park.

Luke's good feelings continued when he doubled in the first inning and Richie singled to give the Yankees a 2-0 lead. The Orioles weren't able to even get a baserunner until the fifth inning. By that time, the Yankees had built a 5-0 lead. Luke cruised to a one-hit shutout, and the Yankees' win forced a rematch for the championship.

While the Yankees celebrated their victory in the dugout, Luke shifted his focus to the next game. He couldn't pitch in the finale, and that worried him. The two teams soon retook the field for the second game. In the top of the first, Luke came up with runners on first and second. He crushed a line drive toward left field. Three steps out of the batter's box, Luke took a peek and saw Michael, the Orioles' shortstop, leap high and spear the ball. Michael whirled around and threw to second base to end the inning.

"I can't believe Michael caught that ball," Luke muttered to himself.

In the bottom of the third, Luke bobbled a grounder, and Michael followed with a double. Two outs later, the Orioles' clean-up hitter, David, blasted a long drive over the left-field fence for a 3-0 lead. Luke kicked the dirt in anguish.

"How did I drop the ball? This loss is all my fault."

In the top of the fourth, Luke had a golden opportunity to make amends. This time he chased a ball over his head to strike out.

Richie could sense his frustration. "Shake it off, Luke. Remember, it's how you respond." Luke composed himself enough to watch Richie blast a double to right-center. Tommy scored to cut the deficit to two and Luke felt a little better.

Neither team managed to score in the fifth inning. The Yankees came up in the final frame needing two runs to tie the game. Luke prayed he would get another chance. Sergio and Devin grounded out, and suddenly the Yankees were down to their final out.

In the dugout, Luke felt despondent. "I can't believe I cost us this game."

"Hey, keep your head up, Luke. You got to believe!" Richie encouraged him.

"PING!" The Yankees jumped up off their bench applauding Tommy's single to left field. Luke pulled his helmet on and sauntered into the on-deck circle. The first pitch to Bryan drilled him in the back putting two runners on base for Luke again.

He could hear his teammates and the fans cheering. "Let's go, Luke!"

"Okay, it's a new at-bat. It doesn't matter what happened before. All that matters is right now," Luke thought while digging into the box. The old Luke would still be furious about his two previous outs and the error in the field. This new Luke was doing his best to stay relaxed and be in the moment.

David, the Orioles' hard-throwing pitcher, wound up and fired a pea toward the plate. It cut outside, and Luke knew it was a few inches off the plate.

"Steee-rike!" the umpire called out. Luke rolled his eyes.

"That ball wasn't even close," he muttered to himself as he took a deep breath.

David rocked into his wind-up, slinging the next pitch even further outside.

"Stee-rike two!" Luke stepped out and glared at the umpire. If David were wise, he would throw another one out there. Luke anticipated David's strategy and crowded the plate. When he saw the next pitch darting outside, he lunged in and flicked his wrist.

"WHACK!" Luke looked up and saw the ball screaming toward the gap in right-center field. "I'm going for three," Luke determined as he exploded out of the batter's box. When he rounded second he could see his third base coach waving his arms. Luke accelerated and slid headfirst into third. He turned his head in time to see Bryan touch home plate knotting the score, 3-3. Luke hopped to his feet and pounded his hands together. David walked Richie intentionally. The strategy backfired when Carter singled up the middle to give the Yankees a 4-3 lead. Finally, Johnny struck out to end the inning.

The Yankees needed three outs, but the Orioles were determined to go down fighting. Michael singled, and Ethan grounded a ball to third base. At the last second, the ball skipped instead of bouncing. It slipped under Jeff's glove and into left field. Luke hustled over and pounced on the ball to prevent any further advancement.

"Shake that off, Jeff. We'll get the next guy." Luke couldn't believe those words came out of his mouth. Immediately, Jeff picked his head up and glanced over at Luke with a bewildered smile lighting up his face. Luke pounded his glove and grinned back. He enjoyed encouraging his teammates.

The next batter hit a sharp grounder to Jeff as well. This time Jeff speared it expertly and raced to the bag to record the out.

"Way to go, Jeff! Great play!" The Yankees' infielders were fired up. David was up next, looking to win the game with a mighty swing.

"PING!" Luke reacted when he saw the ball shoot off of David's bat and head toward left field. He sprinted to his right, jumped, and reached his arm as high as he could. Relief swept over Luke when the ball stuck in his glove. He whirled and threw a strike to Richie at second base, doubling off the Orioles' baserunner. The Yankees were CHAMPIONS! Luke, Richie, and the rest of the Yankees rushed to the mound for a dogpile. After the euphoric celebration, the Yankees shook hands with the Orioles and received trophies. Luke's heart pounded with excitement.

Luke stood in the middle of the diamond soaking it all in after everyone had left the field. He scanned the ballpark for Richie. Usually they hung out after games and discussed what happened. This time, Richie had disappeared.

"That's strange," thought Luke. "Maybe he went home." Luke had never been to Richie's house but noticed he always walked home through the woods just on the other side of the park. Luke decided to run and catch up to Richie.

As Luke got deeper into the forest, he felt like he was further away from civilization. Finally, Luke made his way out of the trees into a clearing and came upon a small gate. Sitting in front of the metal fence was something that caught Luke's eye. He walked up to it and saw that it was a championship trophy just like the one the Yankees had received. Luke glanced around bewildered. There was no sign of Richie. Beyond the gate, he could see hundreds of headstones. Luke realized he was outside of a cemetery. He feared something terrible had happened to Richie, so he raced home to get his mom.

"Mom…. MOM!" Luke yelled between gasps for air.

His mom stumbled out of the bedroom and rubbed her eyes. "What is it, dear?"

"I can't find Richie, but I found his trophy near a cemetery in the woods. I think something happened to him!" Luke had a frightened look on his face.

"Okay, let's call his mother." Luke's mom looked a little worried herself.

"I don't have his phone number, Mom. He never gave it to me," Luke said frantically. "Can you help me look for him?"

She nodded, and they hurried through the woods back to the cemetery.

"Richie! Richie!" Luke cried out when they entered the steel gate. He scanned the plots for any sign of his friend. Off to the right an object caught his attention. Luke and his mom approached a patch of grass to investigate. Slowly, Luke bent down and scooped up the item. In his hand, he held a Yankees hat that matched the one on his head. Luke flipped it over and read the bottom of the brim. "Richie" was inscribed underneath.

"It's his hat, Mom. Where is he?" Luke's voice trembled. His mom didn't respond. Luke glanced at her and realized she was staring at the gravestone next to him. He turned around and followed her gaze. The marker read "Richard Biggio."

"Is this Dad's?" Luke gulped. His mom nodded solemnly. Luke saw something sticking out of the ground. He brushed away some dirt and picked up a photograph. "Mom, what happened to Richie?" he asked as he handed her the photo.

She grabbed it, and slowly her expression changed. "Where did you get this picture, Luke?" she questioned.

"Right here, next to Dad's grave. It's a picture of Richie."

"Luke, this isn't Richie's picture. It's your father. I have all his pictures in the attic. I haven't brought them out because I can't bear to look at them since he died."

Luke was more confused than ever. "That's impossible, Mom. I've been hanging out with Richie for two months. Believe me, that's him." Luke grabbed the picture and turned it over. On the back was a message that read:

"It's not what happens to you in life, but how you react to it. Remember, I am always watching over you, and I'm proud of you.

Love,
Dad"

3

BRANDON

SAMANTHA WISHED HER LIFE WAS OVER. This nightmare had ruined her, and it was only just beginning.

"It's not FAIR!" she yelled at her mother. "Why is he coming here?" Samantha's mom had just dropped a massive bombshell and expected Samantha to be excited.

"Your Aunt has to travel for her job, so we're going to take care of him. I know this will be an adjustment for you, honey, but think of it as an opportunity to get to know your cousin better."

"I don't want to get to know him better. HE'S A

FREAK!" she screamed while slamming her bedroom door shut.

"How can she let Brandon come live with us? He's so annoying and weird," Samantha thought. "I hope he doesn't still talk to himself out loud. Brandon is such a dork. How can Mom let him go to my school? He is going to embarrass me!"

Samantha spent the rest of the night fuming in her room and dreading the arrival of Brandon in the morning. When she finally drifted off to sleep, she dreamt of hanging out with her friends in the cafeteria. While they gossiped, Brandon walked up to Samantha's group and started speaking to himself.

"Oh look, there is Samantha. Should we say 'Hi'?" Brandon paused as if he were listening and then nodded his head. "I agree."

"STOP TALKING TO YOURSELF! YOU MON-KEY!" Samantha sat up in bed screaming. She felt relieved it was only a dream, but she knew the real nightmare would begin tomorrow.

Samantha tossed and turned the rest of the night. Sunday morning arrived much too soon for Samantha, and she was in a foul mood as she got ready for church. Brandon was only 8 years old when Samantha had last seen him a year ago. She didn't think he would be any better at 9. Besides, what 12-year-old girl wants to hang out with her younger cousin, especially a cousin as weird as Brandon?

When Mass was over, Samantha slowly trudged to the car. Her mother tried to cheer her up on the car ride home.

"Maybe we'll go to the zoo next weekend, as a way to welcome Brandon to California."

"The zoo is lame. I don't want to go there. Last time we went there all the animals were hiding except for the stupid birds. I can see birds anywhere.

"Oh come on, honey. It'll be fun. I'm sure Brandon loves the zoo."

"Yeah he probably talks to the monkeys, and they ask him how come he gets to be out of the cage," Samantha chuckled to herself.

"That's not very nice." Her mother tried to stifle a laugh.

In a matter of minutes, their car was pulling into the driveway, and Samantha could already see Brandon sitting on the porch. His light brown hair was cropped close on the sides and a little longer on top. He had grown a little since last year, but Samantha still regarded him as short for his age.

"See, I told you they would be here any minute," said Brandon to the front door.

"He's even weirder now," Samantha thought to herself. "No wonder his mom is sticking him with us."

"Hi, Brandon!" Samantha's mom ran up to him and gave him a warm embrace. A huge smile appeared on

Brandon's face, while Samantha looked disgusted.

"Aunt Terri, there is someone I want to introduce you to – this is Fred. Fred this is my Aunt Terri." Again, Brandon was talking to the front door.

Samantha looked incredulous as her mother humored Brandon.

"It's a pleasure to meet you, Fred. How was your trip?"

"Oh. He says it was marvelous, Aunt Terri. Fred has never been to California. He's really looking forward to staying here. We both want to thank you for having us."

"Certainly, Brandon, we are delighted to have you. Isn't that right, Samantha?"

"Oh yes. It will be more fun than the zoo," Samantha muttered sarcastically.

Samantha locked herself in her room for the rest of the afternoon. She didn't want to deal with Brandon and his wacko imaginary friend. She passed the time reading a book she had gotten for her last birthday. So far it was really spooky, and she couldn't put it down. Soon it was dinner time, and Samantha had to face the music. She dragged herself downstairs and noticed four place settings at the table. Brandon and her mom were already sitting down. Samantha began to take a seat across from Brandon.

"Fred's sitting there, Sammie. We made this spot for you," Brandon blurted out. "I'm sorry."

Samantha glanced at her mom, who gave her a stern look and nodded. Samantha rolled her eyes and moved over to the other seat.

"Okay, let's pray. Dear God, thank you for today's meal, please bless it and us. We want to thank you for letting Brandon and Fred come stay with us, and please watch over all of us in the coming week. Amen." Samantha could not believe how much her mom played into this whole imaginary friend thing. It made her want to puke.

"Here's a piece of chicken and some mashed potatoes, Brandon. Would you like regular salad or fruit salad?"

"I'll take the regular salad, Aunt Terri. Thank you."

"Okay," she said as she scooped him some salad. "What would Fred like?"

Samantha groaned.

"Fred apologizes. He already ate. He would like to enjoy the conversation."

"That's just fine. Let Fred know if he's hungry later we can get him something." She smiled as she began serving Samantha. Samantha just shook her head. "This is going to be a very long night," she thought. Samantha did her best to ignore Brandon's antics during the rest of the meal. She refused to acknowledge Fred and mostly kept quiet.

The next day, Samantha's mom put her in charge of showing Brandon around at school.

"Try not to act like a freak today, okay? I hope you left your imaginary friend at home." Brandon glanced to his left and giggled.

"Oh great, I'm going to have to get away from him as quickly as possible," Samantha thought. "Okay, here's the main hallway. Your class is at the end of it. You come back this way to go out to recess, and your class will show you where the cafeteria is at lunch. Bye." She scanned around to ensure no one had seen her with Brandon.

"Bye, Sammie. Thank you. Fred says 'Thanks,' too. You're the best." Samantha didn't even stop to turn around as she hurried down the hallway.

Samantha couldn't concentrate in school all day. She prayed no one would realize Brandon was her cousin. The end of the day would be the most difficult.

"Meet me at this tree at the end of school. I might be a little late. If I am – WAIT!" Samantha had warned Brandon before dropping him off. If she was responsible for walking him home, then she needed to make sure she was not seen with him. This tree was perfect because it was in the back of campus, and no one would be around five minutes after the bell rang. At least that's what Samantha hoped.

Samantha survived until lunch, but still had half the day to navigate through. Brandon's class had early lunch, and she knew if she got into the cafeteria too quickly she might see him before he returned to his classroom. That would ruin everything. Strategically, Samantha tied her shoes, pretended to have trouble finding her lunch, and then strolled slowly behind the rest of the class on the way to the cafeteria. Slyly, she peeked in the door, but it was too late. Brandon spotted her.

"SAMMIE!" His eyes lit up. Samantha's face fell, and she felt an enormous knot form in her stomach.

"Who is your friend, Samantha?" asked the girl standing next to her with a devious smile.

"Um, he's nobody," Samantha grumbled.

"Hi! I'm Brandon. I'm Sammie's cousin." Samantha covered her face in embarrassment.

"Hi Brandon," all the girls replied in unison.

Brandon beamed. "I'd like you to meet my friend." Samantha knew where this was going and quickly intervened.

"Brandon, you better get to class before you get in trouble."

"Oh, okay. Bye, everyone. Bye, Sammie. Have a good lunch."

Samantha felt a wave of relief wash over her as Brandon departed the cafeteria. She calmly sat down at her usual table and pulled out her lunch. She hoped her friends would not want to talk about Brandon. Of course, that is all they wanted to discuss.

"So, when did your cousin start coming to this school?" Marissa was the leader of the group and one of the most popular students at the school. She always wore the most expensive clothes and spent hours curling her black hair to ensure she looked her best.

"Today. Can we not talk about him?" Samantha wished they would drop it.

"What's wrong with him?" pried Jasmine.

"He's a freak, a sideshow. I can't believe my mom is letting him stay with us for the rest of the year. It's horrible! You have no idea!"

"Brandon seemed nice, and I can tell he really likes you." Camille was always naïve and saw the glass as half full.

"Oh, he is way worse! I don't care if he likes me. I can't stand him. Trust me, you guys wouldn't like him if you were in my shoes. He talks to imaginary friends!" Samantha blurted out and immediately regretted it.

"What?!" Marissa and Jasmine laughed. "He talks out loud to them? What a weirdo. I guess if you don't have any real friends, then that is what you do." They both exploded with laughter. Camille grimaced and shook her head. Samantha felt guilty but joined in chuckling with the other girls. Finally, Melissa and Jasmine moved on to other gossip and rumors. Camille tried to change the subject whenever the girls insulted someone. Samantha, meanwhile, was unusually quiet. She contemplated how to survive this year with Brandon at her school.

The bell rang, and Samantha dragged herself back

to class still embarrassed about Brandon. Samantha was still feeling sorry for herself when school ended, and she had to meet Brandon by the tree.

"Have fun with the weirdo!" Marissa smirked as she and Jasmine left school in the opposite direction of Samantha. "Say hi to his imaginary friends for us." The girls burst out laughing.

"Yeah, if only Brandon were my imaginary cousin," Samantha quipped as she shuffled off.

Samantha cautiously crept around to the back of the school toward the tree. Most of the students had already left campus, and Samantha let out a big sigh of relief when she saw only Brandon standing beside the tree. He seemed to be talking to his imaginary friend. When he saw Samantha, a tremendous smile appeared on his face, and he started waving.

"Hi, Samantha. How was your day? I had the best first day. Fred thought it was great, too!" Brandon was even more excitable than usual, and it made Samantha sick.

"Great. I'm so glad you enjoyed it," Samantha grumbled. "Let's go home.

On the walk home, Brandon proceeded to tell Samantha all about his day.

"My class is so much fun! I made so many friends. I ate lunch with Jerry, Chris, Cathy and Jessica. They were all so great. After we ate, Fred played tag with us. He really enjoyed the class and learned so much from our teacher, Ms. Johnson. I can't wait to go back tomorrow!" Brandon couldn't sit still. It bugged Samantha.

"Good for you. I'm going up to my room," Samantha mumbled as they entered the house.

"Hello to you, too," Samantha's mom said sarcastically. "What's wrong with her?" she asked Brandon after Samantha slogged up the stairs.

"I don't know. Samantha seemed fine on the way." Brandon paused and turned his head to the side. "What's that, Fred? Oh, uh-huh… you think so? I didn't pick up on that, but you are a good judge of character."

"Fred thinks that Samantha was unhappy because we made so many friends and she is not very satisfied with her friends. Fred says they are bad influences, whatever that means." Brandon shrugged at his Aunt Terri as he gave the explanation.

Samantha abandoned Brandon as soon as they arrived at school the following day. She didn't want him to get the idea that they were going to hang out together in public. Unfortunately for Samantha, her friends had other ideas.

"Hey, come on. Let's go see what the freak is doing." Marissa laughed as Samantha approached.

"No, let's hang out here. I'm not going over there." Samantha tried to think of something to change the conversation.

"Well, we are going, even if you don't. Your cousin is too priceless. Who knows what we may see over there?" It was too late for Samantha. Marissa had decided, and Jasmine and Camille were sure to follow. Samantha grumbled but followed the girls over to the younger students' playground. Her feeling of dread increased with each step she took.

"I tagged Fred! He's it!" The girls turned the corner in time to see Brandon claim he tagged Fred. The girls immediately burst out laughing while Samantha cringed.

"Oh, hi, Samantha, do you and your friends want to play?" Brandon stopped in his tracks to invite them to join the game.

"I'm it! Fred tagged me!" A little red-headed girl called out and began chasing two boys.

Samantha's friends laughed again, especially Marissa and Jasmine.

"No, we're good, but can you let us meet 'Fred'?" Marissa could barely contain the smirk on her face.

"Sure! He would love to meet you. Fred! Come here. Samantha's friends want to meet you." Brandon turned towards the tetherball pole and motioned with his arms for it to come over. The tetherball pole did not budge. After pausing for a second, Brandon turned to the girls and motioned to the empty space on his right.

"This is Fred. Fred, these are Samantha's friends. I'm sorry, I don't know your names," Brandon said sheepishly.

The girls broke out in laughter again. "I'm Marissa. Nice to meet you, 'Fred.'" Marissa sarcastically used air quotes.

"And I'm Jasmine."

"I'm Camille."

"Hello, Marissa, Jasmine, and Camille. It is nice to meet you. Fred says he's glad to be introduced to Samantha's friends finally." Brandon beamed.

"Where did Fred come from?" Marissa wanted to see how much entertainment she could extract from this rare situation.

"That's a good question. Fred is from the land of Caelum," Brandon replied earnestly.

Marissa continued to probe Brandon. "Caelum? Is that another planet? Why did he come here? Is he a human?" This was becoming too much for Samantha. Why couldn't the bell ring already? She could already imagine what Marissa and Jasmine's mockery would be like later.

Brandon glanced to his left and giggled. "He's not a human, silly. Fred is a Malach. Caelum is far away, and he traveled here two years ago because I needed a friend after my dad died. He's been by my side ever since. Fred's the best friend I have ever had."

Camille's smile disappeared. "I'm sorry I didn't know your dad died. It sounds like Fred is sweet." Marissa and Jasmine gave Camille a sideways look and rolled their eyes.

"Okay, if he's not a person, what does he look like?"

Now it was Jasmine's turn to interrogate Brandon.

"Well, Fred has six fingers, six toes, sharp claws, and sharp teeth. His face looks like a wolf and his eyes are green. Fred is really tall and has bright red fur with a white belly. He doesn't have any wings, but he can fly. Fred also…" Finally, the bell rang and saved Samantha from this hell.

"Oh yes, that's right, Fred. Let's run to class! Bye, girls. See you later!" Brandon dashed to his classroom, and the girls turned and walked back down the hall.

"Wow, can you believe that freak, a Moron from Wackoville. Where does he get that stuff? Did you hear how he described it? Fred is some weird kind of creature, but not as weird looking as your cousin!" Marissa and Jasmine's laughter made Samantha turn red with embarrassment. She didn't want them to know that though.

"Yeah, I told you he belonged in a circus." Samantha felt sorry for Brandon, but she felt worse for herself.

"You guys, his dad died." Camille tried to shift the conversation. "It's understandable why he would need a friend."

"His dad probably died from embarrassment over having Brandon as his son." Jasmine's words shot a pang of guilt through Samantha. She wished they would stop bad-mouthing her cousin. Fortunately for Samantha, the girls spotted Margaret. She was wearing an old-style dress that looked like it belonged in the 1890s. Jasmine and Marissa quickly shifted gears into mocking Margaret's wardrobe choice.

Later that afternoon, Brandon told Samantha about all the new friends he was making. He sounded like the most popular kid in his class. Samantha couldn't figure out why they would want to be friends with her weird cousin. It must be because he is the new kid. Little kids always want to be friends with new students. Inside, Samantha longed for a simpler time in her life when she was younger. No one cared what you wore, how you did your makeup or hair, or if you were cool. She felt jealous of Brandon and his friends, but she would never admit that out loud.

Brandon interrupted her thoughts when he finally said something that applied to her. "I enjoyed meeting your friends, Samantha. They are so nice."

"If only you knew what they thought about you," Samantha thought to herself, "you wouldn't think they were so great."

"Fred likes Camille, but he didn't really like Marissa and Jasmine. He said they were self-absorbed and judgmental. I don't know why he thought that. I told Fred that Samantha is a good judge of character. She wouldn't be friends with people that were mean." Brandon's words cut Samantha deep.

"Don't ever talk about my friends. You don't even know them," she shot back defensively.

"It wasn't me, Sammie. Fred is the one who said that. Sometimes he is just overprotective of me. I told you, I like your friends."

"Fred isn't real. I know it is you who doesn't like my friends! I'd much rather hang out with them than with you and your imaginary friend!" Samantha lashed out.

"I'm sorry you don't want to hang out with us, Sammie. We will leave you alone." Brandon had a hurt look on his face that only increased Samantha's guilt. She was too perturbed and ashamed to say anything else, so they walked home in silence.

Brandon honored his promise for the rest of the week and kept to himself. This worked out perfectly for Samantha. Although, she might have felt a little guilty about it, if not for the fact that another issue emerged. Marissa and Jasmine were spending more time together alone. When Samantha and Camille showed up, the duo welcomed them, but something seemed off. She and Marissa had been best friends since the first grade and had created this group together. Camille joined them in the second grade but had always been more of a sidekick. Jasmine moved to the school in the fourth grade and within a couple of months had passed up Camille in the hierarchy. Passing Camille didn't bother Samantha, but she would not tolerate Jasmine replacing her! In reality, Samantha had always been number one in this group. Marissa was her co-founder, not the other way around.

"Maybe I'm just paranoid," Samantha thought to herself. This Fred thing had her crazy. She struggled to put it out of her mind for the rest of the day. At lunch, Marissa began making fun of Wendy who sat two tables over from them. Wendy usually ate lunch with Bianca. They were two of the strangest kids in class. Samantha, Marissa, and Jasmine would make fun of the way they dressed and their awkward interactions with other students. Today Bianca was absent, and Wendy looked particularly pathetic sitting all alone at the lunch table staring down at her food.

"Even the pudding doesn't want to be her friend," Marissa chortled.

Samantha joined in on the insults, but her heart wasn't really into it. At least it put her mind at ease. Everything seemed normal again. Samantha continued to enjoy the day, but soon it was time for the dreaded walk home with Brandon.

They walked home in silence, but Samantha could tell something was bothering Brandon. He didn't have the usual goofy bounce in his step and the annoying smile.

"I probably hurt him by yelling at him," Samantha thought to herself. Finally, the guilt and curiosity got the best of her.

"What's wrong with you, Brandon?"

He looked at her despondently. "Nothing." She could tell he was lying.

"Okay, fine. You can talk to me. I don't want you to be miserable." Samantha couldn't believe those words came out of her mouth.

"Well…uh…I guess…um…actually, Fred heard something today, and it upset me," Brandon sputtered. Samantha could see tears welling up in his eyes and her heart thawed a little more. She overlooked the Fred reference because Brandon was in pain.

"What did you hear?" She asked as sympathetically as she could.

"Uh…well…I don't…um…"

"It's okay, Brandon. You can tell me."

"It's just…it's your friends." Brandon was looking at the ground now, and Samantha could see a single tear rolling down his cheek.

"What about my friends?" She could feel herself getting defensive.

"Um…Fred heard them saying some horrible stuff about you," Brandon whispered.

The anger swelled up inside Samantha, but she tried her best to remain calm. "What did they say?"

"I don't want to say it." Brandon stared at the ground.

"Tell me what you say he heard," Samantha responded irritably.

"Fred heard them say you're ugly, your clothes are Wal-Mart specials, and that you are a freak…" the tears were rolling down Brandon's cheeks now.

"What else?" Samantha asked through gritted teeth.

"They were laughing at you, and…uh…they said no guy will ever like you, and, um, your family is a bunch of freaks, too."

Samantha could feel the rage and embarrassment rise inside of her. "Shut your mouth!" she snapped at Brandon. "Don't you ever talk about me like that! My friends would never say that, and Fred doesn't exist! You are the one who is a freak! No one likes you. You have no friends, so you made one up! I wish you never came here! Stay out of my life!"

Brandon's face fell, and he was fighting back tears, but she didn't care. She was so irate that her hands were shaking. Samantha turned away from him and walked more briskly leaving Brandon and Fred behind. She couldn't bear to see Brandon's face anymore. Samantha was ashamed of what she said, and deep inside was worried that Brandon might be correct.

When she reached her house, she scurried up the steps, went inside and slammed the door behind her. Samantha's mother heard the noise and came to the front door.

"Where's Brandon?" she asked.

"I don't know. He's coming," Samantha said without glancing at her mother. She took the stairs two at a time, went up to her room, and locked the door. Samantha buried her face in the pillow to muffle her screams. When she finished crying, Samantha sat sullenly in her room replaying Brandon's words in her head. She thought back on her recent interactions with Marissa and Jasmine. Samantha's over analysis fueled her paranoia and she had a restless night's sleep until the alarm woke her up.

Samantha hurriedly dressed, grabbed breakfast, and headed out the door. She didn't want to see Brandon or her Mom this morning. As far as she was concerned, Fred could walk Brandon to school. Samantha arrived early, hoping to spend some time with her friends and put her mind at ease.

"Hey, guys, what's up?" Samantha pretended everything was normal.

"Hi, Samantha," Marissa, Jasmine, and Camille responded with a smile.

"Everything is okay," Samantha thought to herself, but she couldn't shake the feeling that something sounded different in Marissa and Jasmine's tones.

"Where are your cousin and his friend?" Marissa asked with a smirk that Samantha used to find hilarious.

"I don't know. At home I guess," Samantha replied.

"I thought you walked him to school every day?" The smirk was still there, and Samantha now found it annoying.

"Nope," she replied, glaring at Marissa.

"Okay." Marissa rolled her eyes, infuriating Samantha. She didn't want Marissa to know she was getting under her skin. Usually, they inflicted that feeling upon others.

"So, what did I miss?" Samantha tried to change the subject to the drama going on at school. Marissa and Jasmine exchanged glances quickly.

"You should see what Vanessa is wearing today, and Sean got a new haircut." They started laughing. "It's bad. I don't know what he was thinking. No way Jasmine will ever date him now."

"Like I ever would anyway," Jasmine responded. The girls all laughed, and for a moment Samantha forgot about what Brandon had said.

At lunchtime, Samantha was running a little late and walked into the cafeteria by herself. Marissa and Jasmine were already seated at a table. Bobby and Marcus, two of the coolest boys in school, had joined them today. Samantha had hoped for a long time that Bobby would eat lunch with them. Julia and Kimberly were sitting there as well. Samantha found this odd.

"Probably trying to get into our group," Samantha arrogantly thought to herself. She didn't see Camille anywhere, which wasn't new. Camille often would join them later or eat lunch with other people. As Samantha made her way over to their lunch table, she felt eyes shift toward her. This wasn't unusual either, and Samantha certainly loved the attention.

"There she is."

"Oh my gosh."

"Is it true?"

"I heard it was."

"I always knew she was pathetic." Samantha heard whispering coming from several different tables. At first, Samantha assumed that Margaret must be walking into the cafeteria. She glanced over her shoulder with a smirk on her face. No one was behind her. She peeked to the left and saw that two whole tables were looking straight at her while stifling laughter. Samantha could sense her face turning beet red. She hurriedly shuffled to sit at the table with Marissa and Jasmine.

Marissa and Jasmine rolled their eyes and looked away from Samantha.

"What is she doing here?" Samantha heard Marissa grumble. Her jaw dropped.

"Was this really happening?" she thought to herself. It seemed like a bad dream.

Samantha turned crimson as Bobby and Marcus laughed. Suddenly, like a switch, her embarrassment shifted to anger. She shot daggers at Marissa and Jasmine.

"What is your problem?" she snarled. The boys' eyes grew wide with surprise.

Marissa glared back at Samantha with a smug look on her face. "Everyone knows, Samantha."

"Knows what?" Samantha's voice was rising in anger.

"Everyone knows that you got rejected by Sean, Mark, and Troy. You're boy crazy. It's pathetic, and no one will have you." Marissa's words were like knives shoved in Samantha's back. Jasmine, Bobby, and Marcus burst out in laughter.

"That is a lie, and you know it!" Samantha balled up her fists.

"No, you're the liar! Get away from our table," Marissa goaded Samantha.

Samantha advanced toward Marissa, ready to grab her when suddenly she felt her foot stick. She looked down in time to see that Marcus had stuck his foot out to trip her. Samantha fell forward and landed in a plate of mashed potatoes and gravy. The messy lunch special now stained her new shirt, but she didn't care. Samantha quickly pushed up off the table ready to swing at Marissa, Jasmine, Marcus – or all three of them.

Samantha pivoted toward Marissa and began to lunge for her. She prepared for an all-out fight. In mid-lunge, her body jerked backward. Miss Penny, the cafeteria supervisor, had grabbed her just in time to pull her away.

"Calm down. Calm down, Samantha." Miss Penny's strength surprised her. She whirled around, putting herself between Samantha and the table. Ms. Penny made eye contact with her, and she could see that Samantha was livid.

"Come with me, let's get some fresh air." Miss Penny tried to play peacemaker, and escorted Samantha outside. The students at the table snickered, while the rest of the cafeteria grew dead silent. Samantha wanted nothing more than to push past Miss Penny and tackle Marissa. She longed to use Marissa's face as a punching bag, but she respected Miss Penny too much to do that.

"Okay, what happened, Samantha?" Miss Penny asked when they were safely outside.

"Marissa and Jasmine are spreading lies about me!" Samantha's voice cracked, and her hands were shaking. Tears welled up in her eyes after being so humiliated.

Miss Penny tried to reassure her. "It's okay. You know how our school is; everyone forgets today's rumor by tomorrow." Samantha knew Miss Penny wasn't entirely correct. No one forgot a rumor that quickly. Some lasted forever unless they were proven wrong, or a more momentous event overshadowed it.

"I thought they were my friends. How could they do this to me?" Samantha wanted to crawl into a hole and die. She imagined moving away from school so she would never have to see these people again.

"Do you want me to be honest?" Miss Penny looked into Samantha's watery eyes.

"Yes," Samantha nodded.

"I don't know how you became friends with those girls in the first place. I always wondered why you and Camille would hang out with them. You two always had a good sense of right and wrong, and a compassionate heart. Those other two…" Miss Penny's voice trailed off as she tried to choose her words wisely. "Let's just say they have been challenges. I feel sorry for Marissa because of what happened to her sister, but still…"

Samantha looked down now. "Yeah, I know she misses Caitlin. I can't imagine what it feels like to have a sister die. I just wish she wasn't so mean." She felt ashamed. Samantha knew she behaved just like Marissa, and she didn't have any dead family members as an excuse. Deep inside, she knew she didn't want to be this way. Samantha felt safe being friends with Marissa and Jasmine. They would pick on other people, and thus avoid being targets themselves. She never imagined the situation would turn on her.

"I wish my cousin never came to this school. All my problems began when he came here." Samantha needed a scapegoat.

"I don't think you can blame this on him, Samantha. The way that Brandon talks to you, he loves you like he's your brother. There is nothing more important than family. Those two girls were going to turn on you at some point. They don't care about you the way your family does. If I were you, I'd steer away from Marissa and Jasmine and focus on building friendships with people that have your best interests in mind. Just think about it." Miss Penny always was so wise.

"Okay," Samantha said solemnly. She knew Miss Penny was right. "Can I stay with you until the bell rings? I don't want to go back into the cafeteria today."

"Sure you can, but they aren't going to go away. You are going to have to face Marissa and Jasmine sometime."

"I know. I just can't right now." Samantha realized she wouldn't be able to control her emotions at the moment. They continued to talk for the rest of lunch, and Samantha appreciated Miss Penny's advice. She felt much better and even managed to ignore Marissa and Jasmine's dirty looks when she returned to class. Samantha's mind was distracted all day replaying the despicable things she had said to Brandon since he came to live with them.

"I've been such a jerk to him this whole time, and he's been such a good friend. He's weird, but still a good friend. He's the only one who tried to warn me this was coming. I hope he can forgive me." Samantha's thoughts were racing, and for once she couldn't wait to meet Brandon by the tree behind the school and apologize.

The bell rang, and Samantha jumped out of her seat. Being in a hurry, she didn't notice the snickering of her new found enemies. Samantha bolted out of the classroom and made a beeline for the back of the school. As she turned the corner, disappointment washed over her. No one stood by the tree.

"Maybe I beat him here for once," Samantha silently hoped. Five minutes went by, then 10, and still no Brandon. She knew he would never be this late. "I hope he's okay," she thought as she sprinted home hoping to catch him.

"I'll never forgive myself if something happened to him." Just as this negative thought popped into her head, she caught a glimpse of Brandon up the road.

"Brandon! Brandon, wait up!" she called out.

Brandon paused and slowly turned around. He saw Samantha, and she could spot the pained expression on his face. She knew his feelings were still hurt, and he might even be scared of her. Samantha ran to catch up with Brandon. She could see his eyes grow wide, wondering what she would do.

Samantha grabbed him and pulled him into a big bear hug. "I'm so sorry for the way I treated you, Brandon," she said as tears rolled down her cheeks. Samantha never cried.

The expression on Brandon's face changed. The fear melted away, replaced by his trademark smile. "It's ok, Sammie. I forgive you. I'm sorry that I have bothered you."

"No, you don't have any reason to be sorry. It was my fault. You warned me about my friends. I don't know how you knew, but you were right."

"Fred heard them. I'm sorry your friends treated you that way. It's their loss, Sammie." Brandon embraced her.

Samantha decided to overlook the Fred problem for now. "Thank you. If only my friends would get embarrassed the way they embarrass everyone else." Samantha noticed Brandon get a serious look on his face. He glanced to his left and nodded slightly while a smile flashed across his face.

"What did you do that for?" Samantha questioned him.

"Oh, nothing, Sammie. I think you're right. It would be nice." Brandon had a suspicious smile on his face.

"What is Brandon up to now?" Samantha wondered. The crisis with her friends preoccupied her, and so she didn't give it much thought. They walked together the rest of the way home. Brandon told her all about his day, and Samantha actually tried to pay attention for once. It helped take her mind off of her problems.

Samantha's mom was pleasantly surprised when Brandon and Samantha came through the door. They were engaged in a genuine conversation. Samantha transformed into a polite and patient person for the first time in a long while.

"I better not ask what is going on," Samantha's mom thought to herself. "I don't want this good mood to disappear." Samantha's positive attitude continued for the rest of the night. Surprisingly, treating others well actually helped Samantha feel better and took her mind off her friends.

Samantha felt apprehensive traveling to school the next day. "How can I face those girls and all my classmates again?" she worried. "It's so embarrassing that they think I threw myself at all of those boys."

The pit in Samantha's stomach grew as she walked with Brandon. "This must be what Wendy and Bianca feel every day," she thought to herself. "If I ever get popular again, I will never make fun of anyone," she vowed.

"Hi, Samantha!" She spun around to see a friendly face. She had never been so excited to see Camille. She wished she had treated Camille better all these years.

"Hi, Camille, I'm so glad you're here." The relief on Samantha's face showed.

Camille smiled. "I hoped I could find you before school. It's terrible what Marissa and Jasmine did to you. I told them I want no part of it, and it's wrong."

Samantha's eyes watered. She hugged Camille as tears rolled down her face. "Thank you," she whispered. "I'm sorry I wasn't a better friend to you before. We don't need them." Samantha now had an ally. At least she wouldn't be ostracized entirely at school. Brandon smiled, and she didn't even mind when he embraced her before running off to the playground.

The situation didn't improve for Samantha as much as she had hoped. Camille continued to hang out with Samantha all week, so she wasn't completely alone. Now Camille and Samantha were pariahs together. They were the new Wendy and Bianca. In fact, a few times they ate lunch with Wendy and Bianca.

"See, they are actually really nice, right?" Camille said to Samantha after lunch.

"Yes. You were right. Wendy and Bianca seem like they are comfortable with being isolated, too. They don't even care." The girls' attitude puzzled Samantha. She hoped that one day she wouldn't care what others thought. "It seems like they have so much freedom to be themselves," she observed.

Still, she longed for Marissa and Jasmine to get knocked off their pedestals and receive their comeuppance. The duo's reign of terror had lasted long enough.

A record rainstorm confined Samantha inside all weekend. She listened to the wind and the rain pound against the window while daydreaming about serving humble pie to Marissa and Jasmine. In between these daydreams, she played board games with Brandon, her mom, and "Fred." She couldn't remember the last time she had played a board game, but surprisingly, she enjoyed it. Who knew spending time with your family could be satisfying? She forgot about all the drama at school until Sunday night arrived.

"I wish I didn't have to go back to school tomorrow," Samantha confided in Brandon while they were getting ready for bed.

"I'm sorry, Sammie. Still upset about your friends?"

"Yeah. I don't really care what others think anymore, but Marissa and Jasmine are so smug. They constantly whisper and shoot me dirty looks." Samantha couldn't believe she was pouring out her heart to Brandon. He definitely was a good listener.

"Don't worry, Sammie. My mom always used to say

that pride goes before a fall. We should always treat everyone well. If you get too full of yourself, life has a way of humbling you. Even if it doesn't, they will eventually have to explain their actions to God. I would never want to have that conversation!" Brandon smiled, and Samantha couldn't help but laugh. "Where did Brandon get all this wisdom?" she thought. "Maybe I should listen to what my mom says."

When Samantha woke up on Monday morning, the storm still raged outside. She could hear it pounding on the windows and streaming through the gutters. Samantha enjoyed the sound of rain and hoped it would stay all day long. Unfortunately, by the time she was ready for school, the storm had passed. Not only would she not get to enjoy the rain, but now she would have to walk to school.

Brandon and Samantha employed entirely different strategies when walking to school. Samantha tried to avoid the pools of water so as not to get her shoes or clothes wet. Meanwhile, Brandon engaged in a search-and-destroy mission with every puddle available. He was hopping back and forth from side-to-side stomping his feet as hard as he could. The large splashes Brandon generated shocked Samantha. "How is someone that small able to create such a huge splash?" Samantha thought. Her guilt prevented Samantha from getting upset with him. Besides, she enjoyed watching him stomp water in every direction. Brandon shouted, laughed and talked to Fred as he jumped around. It almost made Samantha want to join him.

Samantha inspected the campus in amazement when they arrived. The playgrounds were full of water, and puddles covered the blacktop. A vast mud pit enveloped the softball diamond turning it into a swamp. Samantha and Marissa had been hanging out at the table next to this diamond ever since fourth grade, and it never flooded this badly.

Marissa, Jasmine and the rest of the popular students had taken up their place at the familiar spot. Samantha would not be going to that bench anymore. Camille and Samantha decided to cross the playground and hang out near the hallway. It had dried out a little bit over there, and they wouldn't be in the vision of her nemesis.

As they walked across, Samantha heard Marissa and Jasmine call out.

"There she goes. I wonder who she is going to throw herself at today."

Samantha whirled around to confront Marissa. Her eyes narrowed, and she glared at the table. Camille tried to pull her towards the hallway.

"Come on, Samantha. Let's go over there. Who cares about them?"

"That's right – keep walking loser," Marissa chided her.

"No. I'm tired of this! I've had enough. She can't keep doing this to people." Samantha had grown weary of hiding from Marissa. The snide remarks and snickering grew louder as she sauntered over to the table. A crowd of students began gathering around to see what would happen between these two former best friends. Samantha clenched her fists. If Marissa wanted a fight, she would be ready.

"Are you just going to run your mouth and tell lies the rest of the year? What's your problem?" Samantha growled.

'You're my problem. It's time everyone finds out what you really are. The secret is out." Marissa smiled. She had an audience, which is exactly what she wanted. "I haven't told them everything, but I will now. What you all don't know about Samantha is…"

Marissa never got a chance to finish her sentence. Suddenly, she found herself launched off the table and into the air. She plopped down face first in the massive mud pit on the softball field, ruining her new dress and shoes. Marissa tried to get up and slipped and fell again. She had a mouthful of the swampy water. Mud covered her face and hair. When she finally stood up, she realized Jasmine, Bobby, and Marcus were all picking themselves up out of the mud pit, too. Now the crowd was bursting with laughter. How had Samantha knocked them all off the table? Marissa couldn't figure it out. She had never been so humiliated before.

The events shocked Samantha as much as Marissa. When the four of them flew into the mud pit, Samantha had still been five feet away from the table. Slowly, a smile spread across her face. She didn't know how it had happened, but she would enjoy every second. Even Camille couldn't help but smile. Marissa, Jasmine, Bobby, and Marcus were too stunned to do anything. They hastily tried to get up and escape the mud pit, only to fall back again over and over. Eventually, they managed to crawl out and slink away to the office to call for a change of clothes.

"See, life has a way of humbling you." Brandon gave Samantha a nudge. Samantha turned around to face him. The twinkle in his eye caused her to burst out with laughter.

"I guess you were right. Maybe I should listen to you more often," Samantha chuckled as she hugged him playfully. "Come on, let's go play freeze tag with your friends."

Brandon broke into a huge grin. "Okay! Let's go!"

Samantha, Camille, and Brandon turned and skipped toward the playground area where Brandon's friends were running around. They left three sets of wet shoe prints in the drying blacktop. Monstrous, muddy footprints could be seen following them. Each footprint had six giant toes with six sharp claws.

4

REFLECTION PART 1

"WHAT'S UP THERE, GRANDPA?" QUES-tioned Ryan as he pointed to the ceiling. He exchanged a nervous glance with his younger brother, Joe.

"Let's go up and find out, boys." Ryan's grandfather smiled mysteriously while he opened the door to the attic stairs. Grandpa Frank's greying hair betrayed his mid 60s age. He was still very fit other than an occasional problem with asthma. He loved pulling pranks on the 10 and 8-year-old brothers. He always had a mystery that involved a thrilling scare prepared for his grandsons. The boys loved going over to Grandpa's house because they never knew what was in store for them. Grandpa had been a principal before retiring a few years ago. He loved making school an exciting place where anything could be possible. Now, he enjoyed doing the same for his two grandsons. They were naturally curious and loved having adventures with Grandpa. Ryan, being the older brother, tried to act fearless in front of Joe.

Grandpa began climbing the stairs and motioned for the boys to follow. He had a small flashlight in his left hand, and when he reached the top, he turned around to help the boys up into the attic. Grandpa installed a floor years ago to make it easier to move around in the large room. The boys could make out several large, spooky objects in the dim light.

"UHHH-OHHH!" Grandpa's favorite catchphrase elicited an audible gasp from the boys. They braced themselves for something to happen. Their eyes grew wide in horror, as out of the shadows a glowing, white figure flew straight toward them.

"Ooooooooooooo," shrieked the eerie apparition. Ryan and Joe instantly jumped behind Grandpa. They knew they couldn't escape, so they closed their eyes and waited for the ghost to pull them back into the shadows and beyond.

"Ha-ha." Ryan slowly opened one eye as he heard his Grandpa's familiar laugh. He saw Grandpa holding the ghost in his left hand, or at least what Ryan and Joe had thought was a ghost. It turned out it was just an old t-shirt with a flashlight inside. They could see Grandpa had rigged it on some fishing line and a motor. The boys laughed.

"Show us how it works, Grandpa!" they exclaimed. Grandpa proceeded to show them the motor he had hidden in the corner and the fishing line. The boys continued to talk excitedly about the ghost until Joe spotted something else.

"Hey, what's this Grandpa?" Joe pulled out a dusty book from underneath an old curtain. The book was beginning to fall apart, and the cover was half missing.

"Be T Sha" it read. Joe began turning the pages and scanning the book.

"Hey, this looks pretty cool! Is it a good book, Grand…ACHOO?" Joe sneezed mid-sentence, sending dust flying.

"I don't know, let me see it." He began turning pages and reading a little bit from the book. "I don't remember reading this book. I'm not sure boys. It does look fascinating…and SCARY!" he shouted. Both boys instantly sprang back.

"Readers of this book, BEWARE!" Grandpa smiled as the boys flinched again. He handed the tattered book back to them. Ryan started turning the pages when something on the other side of the attic caught his eye.

"Is that another ghost you set up, Grandpa?" Ryan expected more tricks.

"It could be, you never know," Grandpa intoned as

all three of them crept closer to the enormous shadowy figure in the opposite corner.

"UHHHH-Ohhhh. Watch out!" Joe slowed down as Grandpa's voice sent shivers down his spine. "What is it? Be careful!" Grandpa warned. The boys slowly approached the massive monster who was dressed in a long flowing robe.

"Ahhhhhhhh!" the boys screamed as the creature seemed to reach out for them. Grandpa burst out with laughter and flipped on a light, illuminating the giant beast. The boys could now see it was a massive mirror covered by a dingy blanket. It stood at least three feet taller than Grandpa and wide enough for three people. The distressed, bronze, décor trim of the mirror would fit perfectly in a haunted house. An inscription adorned the top of the frame.

"Vae qui dicitis malum bonum, et bonum malum." Ryan did his best to pronounce the strange words.

"What does it mean, Grandpa?" Joe asked.

"I have no idea. It must be in another language." Grandpa inspected the mirror closer. "I don't remember this being up here either. It must have been Grandma's, or maybe the previous owner. It looks like there is another inscription down here at the bottom. "Non est verum. Tanquam in speculo considerare velis, ne seducerentur claritatem. Utraque enim nummus habet, ita hic in loco a eros. Hoc enim videtur bene limen viam adtendite autem vobis ingredimini quae egreditur foras?" Grandpa read off the strange words.

"I don't know boys. This one has me baffled." Ryan and Joe tried to read Grandpa's face to see if he could be fooling them again. His face didn't betray any deception. Suddenly the lights flickered off, and the mirror produced an eerie green glow. A strange humming noise emanated from the antique. Ryan and Joe saw Grandpa's reflection turn green. The humming grew louder, and the boys shut their eyes tight. Grandpa's reflection took on a sinister grin. His eyes became fiery red and lightning flashed behind him in the mirror. The boys took a peek and saw Grandpa wink at them. Suddenly the mirror turned completely black. The humming stopped, the attic light turned back on, and the reflections returned to normal.

"Cool!! How did you do that?" the boys asked Grandpa excitedly.

Grandpa gave them a smirk. "I can't tell you those secrets," he laughed. "Come on, boys. It's time to climb back down."

The boys followed Grandpa toward the exit. Joe glanced back at the creepy relic and then hurried to catch up with his brother. He didn't trust that mirror.

"Okay, boys, would you like some lunch before your dad comes over?" Grandpa asked them when they reached the bottom. He closed the attic door with his right hand and flashed a smile at the boys.

"Yes! Grandpa, can we have sandwiches?" the boys exclaimed. They had healthy appetites, and so Grandpa knew he better make them two sandwiches each.

"What kind would you like?" Grandpa asked.

Ryan and Joe exchanged glances. "Salami and cheese like always, Grandpa."

Grandpa got out the bread, salami, and cheese and fixed them four sandwiches total.

"Grandpa, you forgot to cut off my crust. Can I have a knife?" Joe asked Grandpa.

"I'm sorry, Joe. I must have forgotten. I'll do it for you." They wolfed down their sandwiches while Frank worked on his computer. A knock at the door interrupted lunch.

"Now who could that be?" Grandpa wondered.

"It's Dad!" Ryan and Joe excitedly yelled as they ran for the front door.

"Hi boys, did you have a good time with Grandpa?"

"Yeah, it was great! We went up into the attic! It was so cool!"

Rick grinned at the boys. "Thanks for watching them, Dad."

"Sure, no problem," Grandpa replied.

"Is everything okay?" Rick asked.

"Yeah, everything is great now," Grandpa smiled.

"Okay, well we are going to get going. We will come

by and see you later this weekend."

"Bye, Grandpa! See you later," the boys called out as they left. They lived about half a mile away from Grandpa, and so they walked home with their father.

"Did Grandpa seem okay to you guys?" Rick worried about Grandpa. He had breathing problems ever since Rick could remember. Two years ago Grandpa had undergone quadruple bypass after they found major blockages in his arteries. Thankfully, he had recovered well. Still, Rick remained cautious with him.

"Yeah, he did. We had a lot of fun," Ryan said.

"Well, he did forget to cut the crust off my sandwich," Joe groused.

Ryan rolled his eyes, and Rick laughed. "Maybe he just has a lot on his mind. So what did you guys do up in the attic? Were there any monsters up there?" Rick enjoyed the same entertainment that Grandpa did.

"A ghost flew right by us!" Joe exclaimed. "It was glowing and everything!"

"Yeah, then Grandpa showed us how it worked. It was awesome." Ryan loved building things and had a talent for anything mechanical.

"Wow, that sounds impressive. Maybe you can build something like that one day, Ryan. I'm sure Grandpa would help you. What else happened up there?"

"We found a spooky book that said, 'Readers BEWARE,' and Grandpa had a haunted mirror up there!

The mirror scared us the most! It lit up green and made a weird noise. All the lights went out, and I saw lightning in the mirror! Grandpa's reflection turned hideous. It was awesome!" Ryan animatedly told the story.

"I didn't like it," Joe chimed in as he stared at the ground. Rick and Ryan paused.

"What's wrong?" Rick asked.

"It was too scary," Joe whispered.

"That is what makes it fun. I'm sure he showed you the trick. Once you know how it works, then it isn't terrifying." Rick ruffled Joe's blonde hair, trying to reassure him.

"He didn't show us." They could barely hear Joe's voice now.

"What?" Rick asked.

"He said he couldn't tell us this trick," Ryan volunteered. "He pretended he had never seen that book or mirror before. He said it must have been Grandma's."

"Oh. Well, maybe Grandpa has another trick he wants to do with it before revealing the secret. I'm sure he will show you next time. Grandma didn't have an antique mirror. I'm sure Grandpa built it, and this is just part of his story for you," Rick reassured them. It wasn't like Grandpa not to show them how something worked.

"I don't want to see it again," Joe blurted out.

"That's okay, Joe. You don't have to see it again," his father comforted him.

"I do! It's Grandpa's coolest trick ever! I want to know how it works." Ryan eagerly showed his courage.

Ryan continued trying to figure out how the mirror worked on the walk home. Joe tried to forget the petrifying scene he witnessed, and Rick couldn't quite shake the feeling that something was off. He put it out of his mind when they got home so he could play with the boys. Ryan and Joe challenged their dad to a game of basketball. By the time the game finished Mom had dinner ready, and Dad had forgotten his worries about Grandpa.

"Let's say prayers, boys," Rick said as they started to pick up their forks. All four of them made the sign of the cross.

"Bless us, o Lord, and these thy gifts that we are about to receive from thy bounty, through Christ, our Lord. Amen," they recited the meal prayer.

"Did you boys have fun with Grandpa?" Mom asked.

"Yes!" Ryan said. He then proceeded to tell Mom all about the attic. Joe silently ate his food. "Can we go over there again tomorrow?"

"We will call Grandpa, and see if he would like another visit," Mom replied. Joe frowned. "What's wrong, Joe?"

"Nothing," Joe mumbled.

"He's afraid!" Ryan laughed.

"I am not!" Joe shot back.

"That's enough boys," Dad interjected. "There is

nothing wrong with being afraid. Even the bravest people get frightened. It's choosing to act in the face of fear that takes true courage. You don't know how brave you are until you face a situation that scares you, and you reach down inside and do the right thing. It's wise to pray to God for the courage to act, and the wisdom to know what to do."

"Yes, sir," Ryan and Joe replied.

Mom smiled. "Now who won the basketball game out there?"

"We did!" the boys shouted. "At the last second, Joe passed it to me, and I made a layup." Ryan beamed with pride.

"Yep, they defeated me. If you boys stick together, work hard and help each other…"

"We can do anything we put our minds to," they finished their father's favorite saying. Rick loved ingraining the mantra into their heads. Ryan and Joe grinned. Even though they had heard it many times before, it always proved correct.

In the morning, Ryan asked, "Can we go over to Grandpa's today?" The boys were off of school for Easter break.

"He said he would love to have you again for a couple of hours," Mom replied.

"Thanks, Mom!" Ryan said excitedly. Joe didn't appear as enthusiastic.

"You're welcome. After you eat breakfast, get ready, and then we will walk over there." The boys slammed down their breakfast and bolted upstairs to get dressed. The radiant spring sunshine greeted them on the walk to Grandpa's house.

In no time, they knocked on Grandpa's door. After a minute, the door slowly swung open, and the boys peered inside. Grandpa's house sat in darkness, but they could see the kitchen table illuminated by candles. Instantly, the boys braced themselves for one of Grandpa's spine-tingling pranks.

The eerie quiet of the house unnerved the boys. Mom stifled an anxious laugh. She didn't share the boys' love of being spooked. Slowly, they approached the candlelit glow of the kitchen. When they came within 10 feet of the kitchen table, a shadowy figure stepped out from around the corner. Startled, they hastily took a step back.

"Hello, boys." Grandpa's familiar voice had a strange edge. He inched forward, and they could see his face half illuminated by the candles. He had a crooked smirk plastered on his face. "Are you ready to have some thrills today?"

"Uh, yeah," the boys stammered.

"Is everything okay, Frank? Did your power go out?" Mom hoped there was a conventional explanation for the dark house.

"Everything is fine now," Grandpa replied calmly. "I

just wanted to use a few candles this morning. I'll turn the lights on for the boys." Grandpa whirled around and blew out the candles. The sudden blackout caused the boys to gasp.

After what seemed like an eternity the lights flipped on. "Is that better?" Grandpa asked still smiling.

"That's better, Grandpa." Ryan felt relieved, although he would never admit he had been a little fearful.

"Okay, boys, listen to Grandpa and behave. I will be back in a couple of hours. Have a good time. Thanks for taking them, Frank," Mom said as she headed for the door.

"Bye, Mom," the boys replied.

"You're welcome. See you later." Grandpa waved slowly. When Mom closed the door, he turned to the boys. "Do you want to have another adventure in the attic?"

"Yes!" Ryan shouted. His mind had been fixed on the mirror since yesterday.

"No, thank you, Grandpa," Joe replied softly.

"Why not?" Grandpa asked. "It will be exciting."

"I'd just rather play with the toys." Joe told a half-truth.

"It's because he is a coward," Ryan teased his brother.

"There is nothing to be frightened of up there, trust me," Grandpa coaxed.

"I would like to play with the toys," Joe repeated.

"Suit yourself," Grandpa said. "Come on, Ryan, I have more to show you." Grandpa and Ryan marched to the attic door. Joe worried about them, but he couldn't bring himself to go up there. Instead, he wandered to the playroom. Joe half-heartedly played with a few of the robots, but his mind was preoccupied with what might be happening upstairs. He usually enjoyed Grandpa's tricks, but something was different about this one. Joe couldn't shake the feeling that the mirror held a terrible secret.

"It's just your imagination. It's another one of Grandpa's pranks," he told himself. "They will be fine." Joe looked up and noticed a powerful flash of light radiate through the ceiling. He heard Ryan yell, and then Grandpa laughing. Joe trembled with dread. He hoped Ryan had just gotten startled. Joe stopped playing and strained his ears to listen. He detected footsteps descending the attic stairs. They got closer and closer until the door creaked open. Joe heard them whispering, but couldn't make out what they were saying.

The footsteps continued toward Joe until Grandpa turned the corner and entered the playroom. Ryan soon emerged right behind him.

"You missed out," Ryan smiled crookedly at Joe.

"Yes, you did. Ryan had a good time," chimed in Grandpa. "Do you want to go up there now?"

Joe scrutinized their faces for a clue as to what happened up there. They just stared back at him with those crooked smiles. "No thank you. Maybe next time," Joe lied.

"Okay. Next time," Grandpa and Ryan replied in unison. They retreated to the kitchen to talk. Joe felt relieved that they weren't going to force him up there today. Joe strained to hear what Ryan and Grandpa were discussing, but he couldn't make it out.

After what seemed like an eternity, Joe heard a knock at the front door. Feet shuffled toward the door, and then he heard it unlock.

"Hi, Frank. How were the boys?" Joe breathed a sigh of relief. It was Mom. He didn't know why he still felt so anxious.

"They were wonderful, Nancy. We had a great time. Joe is still a little scared of the attic though." Joe turned red.

"I don't blame him," Mom laughed. "Come on, boys. Time to go home." Ryan and Joe followed Mom out Grandpa's door.

"Bye, boys. Don't worry, Joe. We'll go up into the attic next time." Joe glanced at Grandpa and saw that crooked smile staring back at him. He quickly turned his head and didn't look back. Mom talked most of the way home, but Joe didn't hear anything she said. His mind filled with thoughts about Grandpa, the mirror, and the attic.

When they arrived home, Ryan secluded himself in

their room, leaving Joe downstairs by himself.

"Do you want something to eat, Joe?" Mom asked him.

"No thanks, Mom. I'm not hungry." The nervous feeling upset his stomach. Joe fiddled around by himself in the living room for a while. He hoped Ryan would come down so he could ask him what happened up in the attic. A half hour passed by and Ryan did not appear. Joe decided to go up to their room and ask him. He trudged up the stairs and ran down the hallway to the second door on the left. He found it shut, which was a little unusual. Ryan never closed their bedroom door. Joe turned the knob and walked inside.

Ryan had drawn the curtains, and the gloominess surprised Joe. After his eyes adjusted to the dark, he could see Ryan sitting on the bed facing the corner. He wrote furiously in a notebook located on his lap.

"What are you doing, Ryan?" Joe asked as casually as he could muster. Ryan kept his head down and continued writing. Joe scanned the room to see if anything else was amiss. He had excellent observational skills. He always noticed anything out of place. Joe had a near photographic memory. Now he hoped this skill would help him figure out what Grandpa and Ryan had done up in the attic.

Ryan's action figures caught Joe's eye immediately. Ryan didn't play with them much anymore. However, he always would have his figures lined up in a particular order on the shelf above his bed. Ryan often would stop what he was doing to make things exactly the way he wanted them. Ryan always had his Star Wars figures first, then his Transformers, and finally his superheroes. Joe realized they were now in reverse order.

"Hey, Ryan," Joe said much louder than the first time. "What's up with your toys? How come they are backward?"

Ryan paused for a second and glanced up. "It was time for a change," he said and then put his head down and continued writing. Joe noticed he was writing in the notebook with his left hand, even though Ryan was right-handed.

"What are you writing, Ryan?" Joe asked.

"Can't tell you," he replied.

Joe looked at him sideways. "How come you are writing left-handed?"

"Huh?" Ryan glanced up with a puzzled smirk on his face. Joe motioned at his left hand. "Oh, I just thought it would be challenging to practice with the other hand," he said abruptly and then continued to scribble in the notebook.

"It seems like you are pretty good already. You sure are writing a lot." Joe continued fishing for clues. Ryan just nodded. "Hey, what happened up in the attic with Grandpa today?" Joe got straight to the point.

Ryan dropped his pencil. "You should have come up there with us. It was illuminating. Grandpa showed me everything about the mirror. I've never seen anything like it. You missed out."

Joe searched his brother's face to see if he could figure out what happened. Ryan just gave him the same smile.

"Well, what did he show you?" Joe asked curiously.

"I can't explain it. You have to see it for yourself. We will take you up there tomorrow, and Grandpa will show you everything," Ryan earnestly replied.

Ryan always shared how things worked with anyone who would listen, especially Joe. "What is his problem?" Joe thought frustrated.

"Yeah okay," Joe mumbled dejectedly as he walked out and headed downstairs.

"What's wrong, pal?" Dad asked. He could see Joe's long face and slumped shoulders.

"I don't know, Dad. Ryan just seems different," he mumbled.

"Oh, I get it. Well, son, sometimes this happens as you are growing up. Ryan's interests and personality will change, and so will yours. You guys will always be brothers. You need to stick together, but there might be some difficult times as you grow and change. You will get through it. Do you want me to talk to Ryan?" Rick always wanted to help fix a problem if he could.

"No, that is okay, Dad. I don't think it is just a small

change. He seems like a completely different person than he was this morning. Even Grandpa has acted bizarre the last couple days. I don't know what it is, but it seems like ever since we went into that attic…" Joe's voice trailed off because he knew what he was thinking was crazy.

Dad looked at Joe a little sideways. "I'm sure it's nothing. Maybe they just aren't feeling well. You'll see, Joe, this will pass. Do you want to go play catch?"

"Sure," Joe replied even though his heart wasn't really in it. Joe retrieved his glove and made his way out to the front yard. After a few minutes, he began to forget about Ryan, Grandpa, and the attic. He enjoyed playing catch with Dad, and today ended up being no different. Rick loved baseball and threw left-handed, just like Grandpa. He had passed down his love of baseball to Ryan and Joe, but not the left-handed gene.

As they continued to throw, Joe noticed that a figure approached from down the street.

"Hey, Dad, how's it going?" Rick asked Grandpa.

"It's good. I came to check on my family." Grandpa still had the same smirk.

"We are doing well. I'm just playing a little catch with Joe before dinner. Why don't you throw with him, and I'll go see if Ryan wants to join us." Rick handed Frank his glove and headed inside. He examined it for a moment and then slid it onto his right hand. Joe felt unnerved by his mannerisms but reluctantly threw the ball.

Awkwardly, Grandpa lifted his arm up and snagged the throw. He pulled the ball out of the glove with his left hand and reached back. Grandpa's arm motion was stiff and uncoordinated as he let the ball go. It floated toward Joe but landed five feet short.

"What was that Grandpa? Are you messing around?" The words left Joe's mouth before he could stop them.

"Huh? What do you mean?" Grandpa looked puzzled for a moment, but then he quickly added, "Oh yeah, I was just messing with you." He chuckled, and then put the glove down. "I'm going to go see how Ryan is doing."

"Something is wrong," Joe thought to himself. He followed Grandpa into the house and found his parents having a discussion in the living room. Ryan was nowhere to be seen. Joe caught a glimpse of Grandpa going up the stairs.

"Where's Ryan?" Joe asked his father.

"Oh, he said he didn't feel like playing catch." Joe could see the disappointment on his dad's face. Joe just shook his head. He couldn't put his finger on it, but he knew something wasn't right. The attic and that mirror held the key. After about a half hour, Grandpa returned down the stairs.

"You want to stay for dinner, Dad?" Mom asked.

"No, thank you, dear. I have to get home," Grandpa answered as he marched outside without saying goodbye to Joe.

"I'm worried about him. I hope his health is okay." Joe heard his mom whisper to his dad. Joe knew he had to get some evidence about the mirror so his parents would believe him.

During dinner, he began devising a plan. Ryan remained silent for most of the meal, while Mom and Dad discussed remodeling their home. Joe knew Grandpa and Ryan would endeavor to get him up in the attic again. He needed information so he would have to play along. He kept his father's words at the forefront of his mind. "It's choosing to act in the face of fear that takes true courage."

Joe spent the night playing out scenarios in his head. In the morning Joe rolled out of bed and trudged downstairs. He trembled at what he had to do today. Downstairs Ryan sat at the table silently eating breakfast and writing in his notebook. Joe exchanged a look with his Mom to see if she found Ryan's behavior odd. She didn't betray any feelings as she fixed a plate for Joe.

He began eating the eggs she had prepared, and then he heard the words he had been dreading since last night.

"Grandpa asked if you boys want to come over this morning," Mom said as she scrubbed the egg pan. Joe clenched his teeth, but he knew he needed to face his fears to get answers.

"Sounds good," Ryan answered without looking up from his plate. "I'm ready to go now."

"Well, let's wait for Joe to eat and get ready, and then we will walk over there," Mom replied.

"Are you going to come up to the attic this time, scaredy cat?" Ryan chided him.

Joe clenched his jaw again. "Yes, I am." He glared defiantly at his brother.

Ryan looked a little surprised, but then the familiar smirk spread across his face. "Excellent!"

Joe methodically ate his eggs while going over the plan in his head. Ryan adjourned to the other room and pulled out his notebook again. Joe didn't have complete confidence in his plan, but he had to try. He hoped it would help him decipher the mirror's secret.

"Hurry up, Joe. Grandpa is expecting us." Mom rushed him. Her patience had reached its limit. Joe put the last bite of egg into his mouth and brought his plate over to the kitchen sink. He trekked upstairs to finish getting ready. A couple minutes later he emerged from his room prepared to face the music – or mirror to be exact. Ryan lurked by the front door.

"Are you ready, brother? You will love it. This is going to change your life." Joe couldn't understand why Ryan was so excited for him to go up there.

"I'm ready," Joe replied. They embarked on the short trip to Grandpa's house. In no time they were knocking at the door. It swung open seemingly by itself, and Joe could see the house was blacked out just like yesterday.

They crept in and made their way toward the lit candles on the kitchen table.

"Hello, boys. Thank you for coming again. We are going to have fun," Grandpa whispered as he came out of the darkness. It sent chills up Joe's spine. Grandpa had always spooked him with his pranks, but they were invariably in good fun. This time was different, but Joe didn't know why.

"Yes, we are," Ryan replied as he strolled over to Grandpa, seemingly unafraid. Joe turned around and saw the front door close.

"Did Mom shut it on her way out?" he wondered to himself. It didn't matter now. He was on his own, and there was no turning back.

"Okay, boys, let's go," Grandpa whispered as he ushered them toward the attic.

"Time to put my courage to the test," Joe thought. He walked as calmly as possible and scanned the hallway for any other dangers. They climbed the stairs together. A tiny bit of light flickered from under the door. A sense of foreboding overcame Joe when they reached the top of the staircase. Slowly Grandpa turned the doorknob, and the weighty oak barrier creaked open.

"Come on in," he chortled.

"What have I gotten myself into," Joe thought. "This plan is a bad idea." Still, his feet moved forward into the creepy, cluttered attic. Joe glanced to the left and spied the crumbling book they had found the other day. He shifted his gaze over to the corner where Grandpa's mechanical ghost had been.

"I guess Grandpa took that down," Joe thought. "Why couldn't he have removed the mirror?" Eventually, Joe worked up the nerve to scan the back center of the room. The old mirror waited there menacingly.

"Come on over, Joe," Grandpa cackled. "I want to show you something. Actually, this isn't a mirror."

"What is it then?" Joe asked softly. His mouth was dry, and his palms started to sweat.

"To find out the answer, you have to read what it says," Grandpa encouraged him.

"Vae qui dicitis malum bonum…" Joe began.

"NO! Not that one," Grandpa roared. Joe jumped at his sudden change of tone. "Sorry, Joe. You have to read the one at the bottom of the mirror," he whispered again.

Joe peeked at Grandpa and then back at the mirror. His hand reached into his pocket. "Non est verum," he began. "Tanquam in speculo considerare velis, ne seducerentur claritatem," he continued. Suddenly the lights flickered, and the mirror began emanating a green glow. Joe could hear a low humming noise begin. Much to his shock, Joe's reflection began to change. Grandpa and Ryan grinned wickedly.

Swiftly Joe pulled his hand out of his pocket with the small metal flashlight he had concealed there. His thumb flicked the flashlight on, and he pointed it at the mirror. The light did not reflect off of it, just as Joe suspected. Instead, the beam continued on through the mirror illuminating the space behind Grandpa and Ryan.

He did not see a reflection of the attic in the mirror as you would expect. Joe saw a deep, dark cavernous cave, and several sets of eyes peering back at him. Something to the left caught his eye, and his vision shifted in that direction. Joe could make out a figure in the recesses of the cave. He aimed the flashlight toward the rear of the cavern to get a closer look. The beam of light illuminated a short, old lady. Joe's keen observational skills noticed her wrinkled skin and her hair pulled up into a bun. She scowled back at him from behind spectacles. Joe could see her mouth curl up into a smirk similar to the one Grandpa had.

"What is going on here?" Joe thought to himself. The dreadful feeling grew stronger in his stomach, and he felt the urge to escape. Joe reached his hand back and fired the flashlight with as much force as he could muster toward the mirror.

"NO!" He heard Grandpa and Ryan scream. Joe waited for the sound of glass breaking, but it never came. Joe watched in amazement as the mysterious old lady flew toward the front of the cave with both of her arms outstretched and palms up. Joe's flashlight changed direction about six inches in front of the mirror as if it had just struck a wall. The beam switched off. The attic was engulfed in darkness again except for the glowing green light of the mirror. Joe used the distraction to make a mad dash for the exit. Grandpa lunged for him, but Joe was running scared, and they could not catch him. Joe flung the door open and scampered down the stairs. Behind him, he could hear snarls and groans coming from the attic. Joe didn't even glance back as he sprinted out of Grandpa's house and all the way home.

5

REFLECTION PART II

BY THE TIME JOE REACHED HIS HOUSE, HE was out of breath. Joe hastily tried to open the front door, but it was locked. He desperately pounded his fist on it and rang the doorbell. He peered over his shoulder down the street to see if Ryan and Grandpa were still chasing him. Joe didn't see a soul anywhere. The bright morning sun lit up the beautiful houses in the quiet neighborhood. Joe felt relieved to be out of the darkness.

Finally, his dad answered. "Why are you banging on the door? Where's Ryan? What's wrong?" Dad shot rapid-fire questions at him. He could see the concern come over his father's face. Joe tried to answer him, but it was no use. He hadn't caught his breath yet.

"Okay. Take a deep breath, and tell me what's wrong." Rick tried to stay calm so Joe would. After a moment, Joe recovered and told his father what happened.

"Joe, I'm sure Grandpa and Ryan were just playing a trick on you. Let's go over there and talk to them." Rick felt relieved no one was hurt. The way Joe came flying in, he feared the worst.

"No, you don't understand, Dad. It's not a mirror. It is something else entirely. That old lady looked right at me and then flew toward me as if she were trying to grab me. I threw the flashlight as hard as I could. I fired a strike right at the middle of the mirror, and it bounced away without leaving any damage. Grandpa and Ryan were not playing a trick!" Joe was hysterical.

"Come on, Joe. I will be right there with you. We will get Grandpa to explain the setup." Rick's tone of voice comforted Joe. He trusted his dad completely and felt secure with him, so he relented.

"Okay, but be careful," Joe replied as they retraced his steps back to Grandpa's house. When they reached his porch, Rick knocked but no one answered. He pulled out his key to unlock the door. Slowly he turned the handle, and they ventured inside. Darkness enveloped the house. Joe couldn't even see the minuscule illumination from the kitchen candles anymore.

"That's odd," Rick remarked. He flicked the light

switch, but it didn't work. Rick strode over to the window and pulled back the curtains, allowing some light into the house. "Dad? Ryan?" he called out, but no response came. They explored the downstairs of the house but found no clues. Everything seemed to be in its proper place, except for Ryan and Grandpa.

"Let's go check the attic. Maybe they are setting up another prank," Rick suggested.

Joe shuddered at the thought of going up to that chamber again. "Okay, but you better grab a flashlight. It's difficult to see up there."

Rick pulled open a kitchen drawer and grabbed one of Grandpa's flashlights. Joe stayed right behind his father. As they approached the attic stairs, he reached his hand out and grabbed hold of Rick. They hiked up the creaky steps and neared the attic entrance. When they reached the top, Rick turned the handle and pushed the door open. It was pitch black inside just as Joe predicted. Rick flipped on the flashlight and pointed it around the loft. Joe's keen observational skills noticed the book was missing. However, the mirror still stood ominously in the same spot.

"Is that it?" Rick pointed at the mysterious relic.

Joe nodded.

"Okay, let's check it out." Rick slowly advanced toward the mirror. When they were within a few feet, Rick noticed the words written around it. "That looks like Latin."

"Do you know what it says?" Joe asked.

"No. I've seen Latin before, but I've never studied it," he replied. "Maybe we can get Father Bob to come over here and tell us what it says. Non est verum. Tanquam in speculo considerare velis, ne seducerentur claritatem." Rick began reading the words inscribed on the bottom of the mirror.

"No! Don't read it!" Joe shrieked, but it was too late. The irritating humming noise and the eerie green glow began again. "We have to go!" Joe yanked on his dad's arm. Rick looked at the mirror in disbelief but allowed his son to pull him toward the exit. Joe scampered down the stairs, and Rick swiftly followed him. They could still hear the humming, although it grew fainter with every step they took. Rick turned around and looked up at the attic door. He could see the green glow beneath the door. After a couple of seconds, it disappeared, and the humming stopped.

"I wonder if Grandpa and Ryan went out to eat? It's not like Grandpa to not let us know where they are going," Rick asked out loud.

"I have a bad feeling, Dad. I know something is wrong," Joe replied.

Rick looked down at him. He was starting to fear Joe might be right. Rick couldn't shake the eerie feeling that came over him when they were in the attic reading those words. Still, he didn't want Joe to panic.

"I'm sure they will return soon. In the meantime, let's go over and ask Father if he will help us." Rick unlocked the car, and they climbed in to drive down to St. James Church. They had a close friendship with Father Bob Lawrence. He had baptized both Ryan and Joe. They often had him over for dinner. He was only in his mid-30s but had a wealth of knowledge. If anyone could shed some light on the Latin inscription and the mirror, they figured it would be him.

Upon completing the short three-minute drive to the church, Joe and his father hustled over to the Priest's apartment. The small building was located in the back of the property. Rick rang the doorbell and smiled reassuringly down at Joe as they waited. After a few seconds, the door swung open, and standing there was a tall, fit man with a friendly face. Father Bob smiled warmly at them.

"Hello, Rick. Hello, Joe. Thank you for visiting. Won't you come in?" Father Bob welcomed them as usual.

"Hello, Father. It is great to see you, but actually, we are in a little bit of a rush, and we were hoping you could help us." Rick wanted to get right to the point. "We had a little problem at my dad's house, and we think it might be in your area of expertise." He proceeded to tell Father Bob about the mirror.

"Don't you think it is just Frank pulling one of his pranks on you guys?" Father Bob was well aware of

Grandpa's penchant for scary jokes.

"Well, that was what I thought initially, too, but this was unlike anything I have ever seen him do before. I've never experienced that uneasy feeling around one of his tricks. I felt pure darkness and evil. I couldn't get out of there soon enough," Rick whispered in the hopes Joe wouldn't hear what he really thought. "Also, there were some phrases written around the mirror. I think they are Latin. If you can translate them, perhaps they will give us a clue."

Joe could see Father Bob's expression change slightly as Rick gave him more details. A mix of concern and intrigue spread across the priest's face.

"Okay, let's go over there now and take a look," Father Bob said as he locked his apartment. The three of them strode to the car. Joe's father drove over to Grandpa's house. Rick and Joe did their best to fill in the details for Father Bob. As they opened the door to Grandpa's house, Joe instantaneously noticed the darkness inside. The curtains had been shut again, blocking out the sunlight.

Rick opened the curtains for the second time. "That's strange," he murmured with a perplexed look on his face. "I opened these when we were here 20 minutes ago." Father Bob pursed his lips and nodded slightly.

"The attic is over this way." Joe's father led them up the staircase to the upper room. Once inside, Rick turned his flashlight on and started showing Father Bob around the attic. They could feel the bone-chilling cold immediately. Joe hadn't recalled it being this freezing before.

"I see what you mean, Rick. I feel overwhelming darkness here, too," Father Bob whispered to Joe's dad. "Where is the mirror?"

"It is right over there." Rick pointed.

"Ah, let's take a closer look. May I have the flashlight?" Rick handed it to Father Bob, and they all crept closer to the mysterious antique. Father Bob looked carefully at the inscription on the top of the mirror. "Yep, you were right. I recognized this passage right away." Father Bob snapped his fingers. "Isaiah 5:20, one of my favorite Bible verses. Vae qui dicitis malum bonum, et bonum malum. Woe to those who call evil good, and good evil. That's peculiar to have engraved into a mirror. Where is the other inscription?"

"At the bottom of the mirror," Rick replied.

"Hmm…this one isn't something I've seen before. I'll have to piece it together. This first part, non est verum, means 'there is no truth.' You were right to bring me down here. The rest of this reads like a warning, but also a temptation. It's very strange – almost a riddle." Father Bob had a concerned look on his face.

"What does it say?" Joe's dad asked.

"It roughly translates into 'If into this mirror you wish to stare, do not be seduced by the glare. For as a coin has two sides, so too can you into a new place ride. This doorway may seem for you a good route, but take heed when you enter in, what exits out?'" Father Bob translated.

"What do you think it means, Father?"

"It sounds to me like it is a doorway. A doorway to a place you don't want to be – trust me."

Joe felt chills go down his spine. He knew he was right about this mirror, but what did that mean for Grandpa and Ryan?

"Father, what do you think happened to Grandpa and Ryan? They looked into this mirror, and they have been acting strange ever since," Joe asked.

"It is impossible for me to say without seeing them myself," Father Bob admitted. "I fear they could be in danger though. We need to find them as soon as possible." Joe and his father exchanged glances.

"Something else I noticed about this mirror," Father Bob began. "Look at these two inscriptions. They don't match. The style, the size, the texture, they are completely different. It's as if two different people engraved them. The inscription down here strikes me as dark and foreboding. The inscription at the top seems light, almost angelic. It got me to thinking…" Father Bob's voice trailed off. "I'm going to try something if you don't mind." Joe watched as his dad nodded slightly.

"Non est verum," Father Bob began with perfect

Latin pronunciation. "Tanquam in speculo considerare velis, ne seducerentur claritatem." The mirror began emanating the green glow. The terrible humming noise started up again. The mirror started to turn dark black in the background. Joe could see those eyes blinking at him from deep in the darkness.

"Vae qui dicitis malum bonum, et bonum malum." For some reason Father Bob switched to the inscription on top of the mirror. Instantly the mirror stopped glowing green. They could see a soft white light shining out of the edges of the mirror. Even the eeriness they had all been feeling seemed to subside a little bit.

"I've never seen it do that before," Joe blurted out.

"I think it is an antidote put here to protect people from this mirror, a reverse mechanism for this doorway possibly. I'm not entirely sure," Father Bob hypothesized. "This could explain why your grandfather yelled at you when you began reading the top inscription, Joe. I need to read up a little more on this sort of phenomena, and then we need to find Ryan and Grandpa."

Rick and Joe felt much better with Father Bob involved, but their thoughts turned to Grandpa and Ryan. The three of them descended the steps. Joe and his father walked through the hallway. Father Bob lagged several feet behind them still mulling over what he had seen in the eerie chamber. As they turned the corner to go into the kitchen, Rick and Joe were shocked to see Ryan and

Grandpa lurking behind the countertop.

"Hello, Rick. Hello, Joe. What are you doing here?" Grandpa smirked at them.

Rick and Joe instantly stopped in their tracks. Grandpa and Ryan began stalking them causing Rick and his son to take a step back. "Why don't we all go up to the attic? We have something to show you." Grandpa's chuckle frightened Joe. Suddenly Grandpa's smirk turned into an angry frown. "What is he doing here?" Grandpa snarled.

Joe and Rick spun around to see Father Bob standing behind them. Father Bob had his jaw set and was staring a hole right through Grandpa and Ryan. Now it was their turn to backpedal. Father Bob started reaching into his coat pocket for something. Before he could pull it out, Ryan and Grandpa scampered out of the kitchen through the back door.

Father Bob turned to Joe and Rick. "It is what I feared," he said to Joe's dad. "That wasn't Frank and Ryan. I don't know what it was, but it wasn't them. We need to get back to my place quickly." They headed back to the car and drove to the church.

When they dropped Father Bob off, he told them, "Go home and don't let Grandpa and Ryan in if they show up. I will call you as soon as I figure out what we should do."

On the ride home, Dad told Joe, "Let's not tell Mom about any of this right now. I don't want her to worry about Ryan. Once Father Bob figures out what to do, we will let her know. For now, let's tell her Ryan went out with Grandpa, but you wanted to go home."

"Okay, Dad." Joe gazed out the window. He couldn't believe this nightmare was occurring. At home they explained to Mom that Ryan was with Grandpa, but they didn't fill in any more details. Rick read from the Bible while waiting for Father Bob's call. Joe prayed that Father Bob would be able to help Ryan and Grandpa. An hour that seemed like 10 crawled by until finally Joe heard his dad's phone ring.

"Hello, Father. Okay. Uh-huh. All right, we will be right over." Father Bob stood outside with a large suitcase when they arrived at his apartment. He put it into the trunk, and they trekked back to Grandpa's home.

"Hopefully Grandpa and Ryan haven't returned. I need some time in the attic to set up," Father Bob stated flatly on the drive over. He hoped he could intimidate them into leaving again if they were home.

Much to Father Bob's relief, they found no sign of Ryan and Grandpa when they entered the house. The three of them made their way upstairs with the heavy suitcase. Father Bob opened it up and pulled out a Bible, a video camera, a projector and remote, a bottle of Holy Water, a black drop cloth, a flashlight, a strobe light, and a toolbox. As he worked on setting up the equipment, he revealed his plan to them. Father Bob exuded confidence in his plan. Rick and Joe prayed he was correct because he was their only hope.

"Okay, now remember, when the time comes, avert your eyes. I will watch to make sure it works. As soon as I am able, I will cover my eyes, too. No need for all three of us to be at risk," instructed Father Bob. Rick and Joe nodded in agreement. Now they had to wait for Grandpa and Ryan to return.

The wait wouldn't be long. A few minutes later the door opened downstairs. They could hear the sounds of footsteps grow louder. Father Bob retreated to the far corner of the attic with his Bible and Holy Water. He didn't want to frighten them again and ruin the plan. The advancing footsteps signaled that Grandpa and Ryan were ascending the steps. Rick and Joe braced themselves for the confrontation ahead.

Grandpa spotted them right away. He didn't appear to have any difficulty seeing in the dark. "Hello, gentlemen," he cackled. Grandpa's smirk quickly changed into a frown as his suspicions turned to Father Bob. "Where is that priest?" he snarled.

"We had to take him home," Rick lied. Grandpa bought it, and his crooked smile returned.

"Good. Now we can get down to business. Come over here," Grandpa directed them toward the back of the attic. Grandpa and Ryan forced them to stand in front of the mirror as they crowded behind them. "Now read the bottom inscription Joe," Grandpa commanded.

Joe started to recite the beginning of the message. The mirror flickered on, and the humming noise began. The green light illuminated the dark attic. Joe continued reading, "Utraque enim nummus habet, ita hic in loco a eros. Hoc enim videtur bene limen viam adtendite autem vobis ingredimini quae egreditur foras?"

Grandpa and Ryan's crooked smiles became larger as Joe completed the inscription. The humming continued as did the eerie green glow of the mirror. Finally, a bright light flashed in the mirror, and then it turned completely black again. Rick and Joe stared straight ahead with blank expressions.

"Well?" Grandpa asked from behind them. Rick and Joe slowly turned around. They now had crooked smiles upon their faces.

"Finally," Rick said. "I thought we would never get out. Thank you." He chuckled.

"Yes. It's about time. Those two were being quite difficult," chimed in Joe.

"Now we can really get to work," Ryan laughed as he patted Joe on the back.

"What's the plan?" Rick asked. "Who is calling the shots?"

"The Old Woman, of course," Grandpa replied. "She has it all laid out. We are going to finish what she started. Once we tie up those loose ends nothing can stop us. First, we have to take care of that priest friend of yours. With him out of the way, it will be easy," Grandpa boasted.

"Perfect," Rick replied. "Let's put an end to him today."

"Agreed," Joe said. "First, I have a question. Is there any way for them to get out and switch back? I don't want to get sucked back in now that we are free."

Grandpa laughed. "They are trapped. The only way they can get out is if we let them."

"What do you mean?" Joe asked.

"Cover the mirror to be safe, and I will show you," Grandpa commanded.

Joe covered the mirror and wheeled it into the corner of the attic.

"Good. Now that it is safely over there, I'll reveal the unfortunate side of the mirror. Make sure never to repeat these words in front of the mirror. The Old Woman set it up as a one-way portal. She designed it to let us crossover into this world and do her bidding. Unfortunately, a certain unmentionable do-gooder got wind of it and set up a countermeasure for the mirror. As a result of his interference, some of us could no longer pass through freely. Another effect is that if you want the door to swing the other way, you can use the other inscription." Grandpa looked disgusted.

"You mean the one at the top of the mirror?" Rick asked fearfully.

"Yes, but that is only half of it. The Old Woman erased the other half to ensure it could never be used." Grandpa smirked. "She's always one step ahead of them."

"What's the other half?" Joe asked curiously.

"It's, Vae qui dicitis malum bonum, et bonum malum. Lux in tenebris lucet, et tenebrae eam non comprehenderunt. It's my least favorite phrase to hear, such nonsense," Grandpa growled.

While Grandpa was talking, he did not notice Father Bob quietly wheeling the mirror out of the shadows behind him. Father Bob removed the cover that he had draped over the mirror. Immediately upon Grandpa finishing the inscription, bright light radiated throughout the attic. Grandpa and Ryan whirled around in shock.

"What did you do?!" Grandpa shouted.

"Close your eyes, Joe!" his father yelled. Joe immediately shut his eyes tightly. Grandpa and Ryan tried to turn away from the mirror to escape. Father Bob and Rick spun them back around and held them in place. The light continued to get brighter, and a peaceful melody filled the room.

"Okay, Rick, turn away from the mirror now," Father Bob shouted.

Rick let go of Grandpa for a moment and picked up the blanket that had been concealing the mirror. "Sorry, Bob, but I have to do this. Watch over my family for me." Rick threw the blanket over Father Bob and pushed him out of the way. He secured Grandpa and Ryan's heads to prevent them from avoiding the mirror's light.

"No!" Father Bob yelled as he struggled to get out of the blanket, but it was too late. The light grew brighter, followed by a tremendous flash, and then it was gone. The mirror returned to black. Father Bob removed the blanket and scanned the room. Joe still crouched down closing his eyes. Grandpa and Ryan lay unconscious on the floor and Rick had collapsed behind them. Father Bob covered the antique again. In the corner, sat the projector screen Father Bob had used to set up a fake mirror. It had fooled Grandpa and Ryan into thinking they had switched Rick and Joe.

Father Bob scrambled over to Joe and helped him up. He then moved over to check on Grandpa and Ryan. They started stirring and rolled over. Ryan put his hand to his head as if he had a headache, while Grandpa blinked and rubbed his eyes. The evil smirks had vanished from their faces. Rick slowly stumbled to his feet as well.

"Frank?" Father Bob asked cautiously.

Grandpa turned towards Father Bob. "Thank you, Father. I thought we would never get out of there." Father Bob breathed a sigh of relief. He instantly knew the man standing before him was indeed Grandpa.

"Are you okay, Ryan? Where were you two? Do you remember anything?" Joe had lots of questions.

"I remember everything," Ryan responded.

"We were trapped in a dark cave with hissing sounds

all around us. We could see you every time this mirror came on, but we had no way to get out," Grandpa replied. "I felt a sense of despair there. She's planning something big. We have to stop her."

"Do you have any idea what she's planning?" Rick asked his father. Grandpa shook his head.

"You never should have pushed me out of the way, Rick. It was too risky. You have to take care of your family," Father Bob interjected.

"I know," Rick replied sheepishly. "It felt like something I had to do though. The imposters said they needed to get rid of you for their plan to work. I didn't want them to win."

"Well, fortunately, it worked out well, and we are all safe. Thank you." Father Bob shook Rick's hand.

"What do we do now? We can't just wait for her to make her next move," Grandpa implored Father Bob.

"I'm not sure. I'll need to do some research. Do you mind if I borrow this mirror?" Father Bob inquired.

"Not at all, I want it as far away from my house as possible." Grandpa was still shaken up. "Be careful though, Father. It opens the door to a very evil place. I recognized some poor souls there, and some very evil ones."

"Who did you see there?" Father Bob asked.

"Do you remember when you helped me through all the guilt I had?" Grandpa reminded him.

"Yes, of course, Frank."

"Well, I saw her," Grandpa whispered.

"Are you sure?" Father Bob looked serious.

"I will never forget her face. It was Mrs. Yorp. I could smell the smoke the same as that day." Father Bob stared at him in disbelief.

"She's the one who is planning something big, I felt so helpless again in there, and it brought me right back to that awful day. Captain Richard was trapped there, too." Grandpa's eyes filled with tears.

"Who is Mrs. Yorp?" Joe asked.

"Who is Captain Richard?" Ryan asked.

"What are you talking about, Dad?" Rick asked Grandpa.

Grandpa just shook his head. "I can't tell them, Father." He choked on his words.

"Your grandfather used to be a principal of an elementary school. During his second year as principal, he had a teacher named Mrs. Yorp on his staff. One afternoon, she locked her class inside the room and lit the whole place on fire. Grandpa did everything he could to rescue those children. Captain Richard rushed to the school in an attempt to help. Unfortunately, none of the students made it out. Captain Richard got caught in the blaze as well. Your grandpa barely made it out alive. The whole community was devastated as you can imagine." Rick and the boys were mesmerized as Father Bob recounted a story they had never heard before.

"Is that why you sometimes have trouble breathing Grandpa? I just thought you were old." Ryan immediately covered his mouth after realizing how it sounded.

Grandpa smiled wistfully. "Yes," he nodded. "I saw Captain Richard inside the cave and all the little girls and boys from Mrs. Yorp's class. Captain Richard told me they had been trapped in the cave ever since that terrible day." Grandpa gazed off into the distance. "Can you imagine what it must be like to be trapped all this time?"

Father Bob made the sign of the cross and said a little prayer. "Did Captain Richard tell you anything else?"

"Well, he told me Mrs. Yorp leaves the cave sometimes. I don't think she is trapped there like the rest of us," Grandpa speculated.

"Is she the short, old woman with the spectacles?" Joe asked.

"Yes, that's her," Grandpa responded.

"She's the one who protected the mirror when I threw the flashlight at it," said Joe.

"I would imagine she has the power to come and go as she pleases," Father Bob chimed in. "I'm going to go study this mirror and see what else I can discover. With any luck, I'll be able to help everyone trapped in that cave.

"Yes, hopefully, we can help them," Rick agreed. "Let us know what you decide to do, Father. We want to help you every step of the way."

"I've been waiting 30 years to make up for that day."

Grandpa's steely eyes and clenched jaw revealed his determination.

"I will. You can count on it. We need to work together to defeat her." Father Bob nodded. The three men carried the evil relic down the stairs so Father Bob could take it to his apartment.

"Do you mind giving me a ride home, Frank? The mirror should be easier to transport in your van," Father Bob explained.

"Sure, no problem. I'll help you load this thing into the van, just do me a favor and keep it covered." Grandpa grinned. "Rick, do you mind grabbing my keys? They are on the kitchen counter."

"I'll get them and meet you outside," Rick replied. "Let's go, boys, we're going to head home, too." Ryan and Joe followed their dad into the driveway. Father Bob and Grandpa carefully set the concealed mirror down next to the van.

"Go ahead and throw me the keys, Rick." Grandpa waved his hand. Rick expertly threw the keys to Grandpa who snatched them out of the air. "Thank you. I'll come by later," Grandpa suggested as he climbed into the van.

"Sounds good. Come on, boys." Rick unlocked the doors. Ryan and Joe piled into the backseat. Frank and Rick pulled away from Grandpa's house and headed in opposite directions down the road. Joe peered out the window deep in thought.

After a moment he turned to Ryan. "Did you see that, Ryan?" he whispered.

"See what?" Ryan spoke in hushed tones, too.

"Dad threw the keys to Grandpa with his right hand." Joe leaned closer.

"So what?" Ryan questioned his brother.

"Dad is left-handed. He never throws with his right hand." Joe's worried expression unsettled Ryan.

"I'm sure you just imagined it. I didn't notice anything different." Ryan tried to reassure his brother.

"No. Trust me," Joe said adamantly. "It's just like when you and Grandpa were switched. Everything was opposite. That isn't Dad."

6

FATHER BOB

FATHER BOB SAT ISOLATED IN THE DEN OF his apartment. Laid out before him were piles of well-organized books on his oak table. His own book, 'Faith of Our Fathers,' sat off to the side. He had written it a year ago, but it would not be helpful with his current predicament. Father Bob turned his attention to the other books. In one stack alone were a host of books on documented miracles, Saints, church teaching, and unexplained mysteries. He currently thumbed through a book written by a priest about spiritual warfare. Father Bob took copious notes and had a top-notch memory.

He hoped to find some reference to a mirror or a portal. He needed some type of clue that could help him rescue the poor souls trapped in Mrs. Yorp's cave.

"Help them. Help them." Father Bob looked up from his book upon hearing a whisper. He scanned around his apartment but observed nothing out of order.

"Must be my imagination," he thought to himself.

"Help them. They need your help," Father Bob heard the whispering again.

"Hello? Who is there?" he called out to the empty apartment.

"Hello, Brandon." Now the voice was clear.

"Brandon? I have not heard that name in a very long time," Father Bob replied. "Who is there? Your voice sounds familiar."

Out of the shadows of the den a large figure appeared. He had six fingers and six toes. The creature's wolf-like face had razor-sharp teeth. The towering figure broke out into a broad smile, and his green eyes twinkled in the darkness. The creature's eyes portrayed a friendliness that Father Bob recognized at once.

"Fred? What are you doing here? I haven't seen you since junior high school. I almost thought you were part of my childhood imagination." Father Bob gave Fred a big embrace.

"I've still been watching over you, but you haven't needed me, Brandon. Now, things have changed." Fred's smile faded. "We have been preparing you for this moment. I'm here to relay messages and help you as much as I can, but you must make some difficult decisions."

"Does this have to do with the mirror?" Father Bob asked.

"Yes, but that is only a small part of it. There are many pieces to the puzzle. Some I can reveal to you, some you must figure out on your own," Fred continued. "First, I no longer need this form. It was helpful for you as a child." Fred transformed into an Angel. "God has an important mission for you, Brandon. Do you accept?"

"I will. Please help me to understand, Fred." Brandon knelt before him.

"A great battle is coming, one that plays an integral part in the eternal war of good versus evil. You must gather others for this conflict." Brandon listened intently.

"Okay, who else do we need?"

"You will need Samantha, and her friend Marissa,"

Brandon looked quizzically at Fred. "I can call Samantha, but I don't think she has spoken to Marissa in years."

"Trust me," Fred replied. "There is a man named Luke and a woman named Ashley. I will give you details on where you can find them. Frank, Rick, Ryan, and Joe are also needed."

"I know they will want to do whatever they can to stop Mrs. Yorp. How do the others fit in?" Father Bob questioned Fred.

"I'm sorry. That is something you will have to figure out for yourselves. It must be this way for the good of everyone. I have given you what is necessary at this time. After you contact the others, there is one more child who requires your help. She is in grave danger, so you must hurry," Fred's tone conveyed the direness of the situation. "I will return," Fred whispered before he vanished.

"Let's roll," Father Bob whispered as he grabbed his belongings to head out the door. Unfortunately, he did not notice that in the corner of his apartment, Grandpa's mirror was glowing green, and an old, sinister face was peering out of it with an evil smile.

7

THE LIBRARY

BREELYN RACED AS FAST AS HER SLENDER, 10-year-old legs could move. She could hear screaming and yelling behind her, but still, she continued on. Behind her, three irate, hulking individuals gave chase. She glanced up and spied another imposing figure blocking her path.

"Between a rock and a hard place," Breelyn thought to herself. "Time to go." Breelyn expertly took an explosive touch on the soccer ball, pushing it toward the lanky girl in front of her. Only moments before the defender would have a shot at the ball, Breelyn cut inside with the outside of her left foot. Just like that, she was beyond the last line of defense and nothing but green grass, the goalie, and the goal in front of her.

"Go, Breelyn, go!" The shouting from the sideline grew louder. The four beaten girls gave chase, but they had zero chance of catching Breelyn. She closed within 20 yards of the goal and began visualizing where she would drill the ball. Breelyn took a quick peek up and eyed the hapless goalie indecisively standing in front of the goal. "Lower, left corner," she thought as she looked down at the ball.

After one more touch, Breelyn lifted her head and readied her left foot to fire a rocket toward the goal. The shot never materialized. Breelyn hesitated for a moment because the previous goalie had vanished. A short, elderly woman with spectacles and her hair pulled into a bun had somehow substituted for Breelyn's other victim. The hunched over lady glanced up and smiled. In a flash, she flew towards Breelyn, knocking the ball away.

"Beep! Beep! Beep!" Breelyn rolled over and hit her alarm clock. "What a strange dream," she thought before rolling back over in her warm bed. Next to soccer and reading, sleeping was Breelyn's favorite past time right now. It was a little peculiar for a 10-year-old girl, but she didn't care. She loved her sleep. "Just five more minutes," she thought as she closed her eyes. Thirty minutes later Breelyn glanced up to see the clock. She groaned and kicked off her covers. Even though it was Saturday, she didn't want to sleep in past 8:30. The library opened at 9, and Breelyn sought to pick out a new book before her soccer game in the afternoon.

She dragged herself to the bathroom and got ready as quickly as she could move at this point in the morning. Breelyn hurried downstairs to grab a little breakfast before venturing to her sanctuary. Her mother had already been at her job for an hour. She worked six days a week trying to offset the fact that Breelyn's dad had left them eight years ago. Breelyn admired her mother's work ethic, but secretly wished they could spend more time together. Her mom didn't show Breelyn affection very often and could be quite critical. Consequently, Breelyn had developed a very stubborn, hard-working personality as well. Books and soccer became her emotional outlets.

A short trek delivered Breelyn to the two-story stone building soon after it opened. She loved sports books, but mysteries were her favorite. "I hope they have one I haven't read yet." Breelyn skipped toward the mystery section but was dismayed to see it was no longer there.

"It's so annoying when they move things around," Breelyn thought as she approached the librarian at the front desk. The usual lady that worked on Saturdays was not at the counter.

"Excuse me, ma'am," Breelyn began. "Can you tell me where the mystery section is, please?"

The new librarian smiled warmly, and her brown

eyes twinkled. She appeared to be in her mid-40s, with a slender build and average height. Her brown hair was cropped to shoulder length. Breelyn knew all the librarians' names because she came in so often, but she did not recognize this one. She read the new lady's name tag: Ms. Ignis.

"You like mysteries, huh?" the librarian chuckled. "Why don't you try this one?" Ms. Ignis brought a book out from under her desk. Breelyn stared at the brand new novel. It was a paperback, and Breelyn could see the cover had some shadowy figures on it. She got chills just looking at the book and loved it instantly.

"I'll take it!" Breelyn blurted out enthusiastically.

"Very good." The librarian's eyes twinkled. Breelyn began to get out her library card. "Oh, it's not in the system. Actually, this is one of my books. You can have it, as a gift. I always like to encourage young readers." She smiled a warm, lopsided smile.

"Thank you so much, Ms. Ignis!" Breelyn murmured on her way out the door.

"You're welcome, child," the librarian whispered.

Breelyn clutched her new prized possession tightly as she danced all the way home. She couldn't wait to begin reading the novel. With an hour of free time before she had to get ready for her game, Breelyn flipped open the book and plopped down on the couch. The book immediately captured her interest. The main character was

Allie, a soccer player who didn't have a father, just like Breelyn. It was an easy read, and Breelyn became enthralled with each page. Allie's team had been struggling during the season, even though Allie had been playing really well. One day, a mysterious girl showed up to play on Allie's team. No one knew where she was from, but they were impressed with her soccer skills. Allie began to feel jealous of the new girl.

Breelyn finally glanced up at the clock and realized it was time for her to go to the game. "Just when this was getting really good," she complained. Hastily, she dressed for the game and made her way out the door. On her walk to the game, Breelyn began thinking about her team, The Force. They hadn't been winning many games this season. It killed Breelyn – she loathed losing. It's probably why she enjoyed reading more this year.

"We better win today," she told herself. "The Mustangs aren't very good either. If we can't beat them, we should just cancel the season." When she reached the field, the team was already warming up for the game.

"Hustle up, Breelyn, you're late," Coach Zylker yelled out. Breelyn sprinted over, put down her bag and started warming up with the team.

Eventually, game time arrived, and Breelyn felt locked in. The match began well for The Force, as they controlled the ball and had possession in the Mustangs' side of the field for the majority of the first half. The

Mustangs kept three defenders back to try to prevent Breelyn from scoring. Breelyn had a couple of nice shots from outside of the penalty box. One missed just inches wide, and the other was stopped by a nice save from the goalie. About five minutes before halftime, The Force lost the ball near midfield. The Mustang player sent a long ball down the left side toward a striker. The Force's goalie hesitated near her own goal for a couple moments and then tried to come out to get the ball. It was too late. The Mustang striker placed the ball around her and into the far right corner of the goal. Just like that, it was 1-0 at halftime.

Breelyn hung her head while dragging herself off the field. She had seen this all before. It was just like the previous four games. The Force would play pretty well for a while and then fall apart. Breelyn glanced up while Coach Zylker was talking and noticed a new girl walking up to the team. She wore a Force uniform, but Breelyn had never seen her before.

"Coach," Breelyn interrupted, nodding toward the new girl. Coach Zylker stopped and turned around.

"Oh, hello, Chloe, I wasn't sure if you were going to make it today. Girls, this is Chloe. She just moved here and is going to be on our team for the rest of the year.

"Hi," Chloe smiled shyly.

"Hello, Chloe," the girls replied less than enthusiastically.

Coach Zylker shot the girls a look to encourage them to be more welcoming. Before the girls could respond, the referee blew his whistle indicating it was time for the second half. The girls trotted out to the field hoping to even the score. Unfortunately for The Force, the second half began much the same way as the first half ended. The Mustangs got a quick steal, passed the ball up to their best striker, and she put it over the goalie's head for a 2-0 lead. Breelyn kicked the grass in disgust.

Coach Zylker, perhaps out of desperation, subbed Chloe in for Sara, the Force's center midfielder. "What is he doing?" Breelyn thought. "Why is he taking out one of our best players for the new girl? I can't wait until this game is over."

Breelyn passed the ball back to Lucy, the other center mid. She wasn't going to take a chance with the novice girl. Lucy promptly lost the ball. The Mustang player turned to send a pass up to the striker, but Chloe flashed in and stole the ball. She took a couple of dribbles and played a ball out wide to Caroline on the wing. Caroline made a beeline down the sideline and then crossed the ball into the middle for Breelyn. After receiving the pass, she spun around the defender and headed toward goal. As usual, the Mustangs had three defenders in her path, and Breelyn didn't have a lane to shoot. Out of the corner of her eye, she saw Chloe sprinting towards the opposite side of the box.

"Okay, let's see what you can do." Breelyn reluctantly passed the ball to Chloe. She took one touch to settle the pass, and then Chloe drilled a shot into the top corner of the goal! Just like that, it was 2-1, and The Force had life. Breelyn watched as all of her teammates congratulated Chloe.

"Nice shot, Chloe," she muttered, unimpressed. Five minutes later, Breelyn pressured a Mustang defender and stole the ball from her 10 yards outside of the penalty box. Deftly, she cut inside the remaining defender and expertly placed a low, right-footed shot into the near corner to tie the game.

"How about that, Chloe?" she thought as the team congratulated her on the shot.

"Great job, Breelyn! Now let's get another one!" Chloe patted her on the back.

"Thanks. Yeah! Let's go!" Breelyn realized maybe she had misjudged Chloe.

With time winding down in the second half, Chloe dispossessed a Mustang player near the half line and quickly turned upfield. She made a move to get past a defender, but still had two opposing players between her and the goal. Breelyn anticipated Chloe running into trouble and sprinted up the other side of the field. Chloe instantaneously caught sight of her and drilled a perfect pass on the ground towards Breelyn. Two touches later, the ball was in the back of the net. The Force had a 3-2 win, and Chloe and Breelyn were exchanging high fives, hugs, and smiles. It was the most enjoyment Breelyn had during a soccer game in a long time. Exuberantly, she floated all the way home.

Breelyn kept replaying the epic comeback in her mind until she caught sight of her book on the coffee table. Breelyn settled in to do some more reading. As she cracked open the book, she recognized how similar today's game was to the book.

"How bizarre," she thought. "I wonder if they win like we did." Breelyn continued reading. In the book, Allie's team quickly found themselves behind 2-0, paralleling Breelyn's game earlier. In the second half, the new mystery girl scored a goal to make it 2-1. Breelyn ascertained that Allie was conflicted by many of the same feelings she had today, chief among them jealousy. Breelyn's arms lit up with goosebumps due to the eerie resemblance between this book and her life. Sitting alone in her house, Breelyn almost lost her nerve and wanted to cease reading, but she felt compelled to find out how it ended.

Allie delivered the second goal to her team, precisely as Breelyn had earlier. Allie felt vindicated but was taken aback when the mystery girl congratulated her. Eventually, the chapter concluded with the mystery girl making a brilliant pass to Allie, who scored the winning goal. The girls celebrated and were on their way to becoming great friends. Breelyn paused for a second and scanned the room.

"How could this be happening?" she thought. "Was this just a crazy coincidence? Did someone replace my book after the game as a prank?" Breelyn obsessed about where the story would lead next, so she continued reading. The mystery girl disappeared and did not come to the following game. Allie's team lost, and her coach and teammates claimed they had never heard of or seen the mystery girl. It drove Allie crazy as she tried to solve the mystery.

"Okay, that other chapter was just a coincidence. No way will that happen with Chloe. That doesn't happen in real life." Breelyn felt relieved. She relaxed and delighted in reading more of the story. She appreciated spooky tales, with unpredictable twists. However, Breelyn didn't want to experience them in real life.

"Allie was perplexed. She hadn't dreamt about the comeback win the other day and the mystery girl showing up to help them win. She wasn't insane. Why couldn't anyone else remember?" Breelyn read faster to find out what would happen to Allie.

"Allie opened up her soccer bag and found a note. It read, 'She was real. You're not crazy. You can find her at the library, hurry.' Allie looked around her house.

'Where did this note come from?' she wondered. Allie hurriedly got ready and headed to the library to solve the mystery."

The suspenseful book enthralled Breelyn, and she

couldn't put it down. Allie reached the library only to find it a ghost town. She began searching for the new girl, or another clue.

"WHAM!" Out of nowhere, a door slammed shut, Breelyn jumped and nearly hit the ceiling. In a flash, she whirled around.

"Jumpy are we?" her mother laughed as she came into the living room. Breelyn had been so focused on the story, that she hadn't heard her mom open the door.

"It's this story," Breelyn chuckled now, too. "It's amazing, but eerie."

"Well, don't read it if it is terrifying." Her mom didn't exactly encourage her reading habits. "Why don't you take a break from it and help me make dinner?"

"Okay Mom," Breelyn replied reluctantly. She wanted to find out what happened to Allie but respectfully assisted her mom with dinner. Breelyn rarely got attention from her mom, so she endeavored to please her whenever possible.

Unfortunately for Breelyn, she couldn't find time to discover more about Allie's adventure. By the time dinner was made, eaten, and cleaned up, it was late. She was forced to get ready for bed. Breelyn had another vital game early tomorrow morning, and so she prioritized a good night's sleep.

She slept like a rock and woke up feeling refreshed. Breelyn's positive mood continued as she made herself some breakfast and thought about the game today. She couldn't wait to get to the soccer field and see Chloe again. This level of excitement hadn't been a part of her life for a long time. Breelyn briskly dressed in her soccer uniform, grabbed her soccer bag, and dashed all the way to the field.

Caroline was already at the field, but Breelyn was the second player to show up. They chatted about school and the game while they waited for more players to arrive. One by one, more girls trickled in, and they began to pass the ball around while they talked. Finally, the coach arrived, and they were only missing two girls, Brittany and Chloe. Breelyn longed to warm up with Chloe and get to know her better. She believed they could really be dynamic on the field together for The Force.

Thirty minutes before kickoff, Brittany finally showed up. Typically, she was the last one to arrive. Breelyn was pleased to see her but kept scanning the parking lot for Chloe.

A few minutes later, she walked over to Coach Zylker. "Hey Coach, is Chloe coming to the game today? It's almost game time."

Coach Zylker was busy filling out his roster. "Who?" he looked up, perplexed.

"Chloe, the new girl from last game," Breelyn reminded him patiently. Coach Zylker could be a little absent-minded.

"What are you talking about, Breelyn? We don't have a new girl. We have the same 16 girls we have always had." Coach Zylker shook his head as he went back to writing his roster. Breelyn peeked over his shoulder at the list. Sure enough, it was the 16 names she had seen all season. Chloe's name was nowhere on the sheet.

"But she was at last game. She scored a goal. She assisted one of my goals. How can you not remember?" Breelyn was irritated. This was not amusing, and she had anticipated playing with Chloe today.

"Breelyn, you scored three goals yesterday, unassisted. I'm not in the mood for these jokes. We have another game today. Get focused. Another hat trick would be great. Now go finish your warmup." Coach Zylker waved her off.

Bewildered, Breelyn returned to the field. "What is going on here?" She pondered the mystery until she recalled her book. Breelyn retreated to the bench to search for a note in her bag. Dishearteningly, there was none. Dejectedly, Breelyn trekked onto the pitch to begin the game.

Unfortunately for The Force, Chloe's disappearance had Breelyn utterly unfocused on the soccer game. She had her worst performance in the history of her soccer career. Coach Zylker even substituted her out of the game with 15 minutes remaining.

"Wish the real Breelyn would have shown up today," he muttered as she moped to the bench. The Force lost 5-0, and Breelyn dragged herself home. Everything appeared bleak at the moment to Breelyn. All the excitement from this morning faded away. She sullenly marched into her house, tossed her bag down and plopped onto the couch. After laying there for a few minutes, she rolled over to get her uniform out so she could throw it into the washing machine.

Breelyn pulled the jersey and shorts out and then noticed something fall off to the side. It was a note! Slowly, Breelyn unfolded the paper.

It read, "She was real. You're not crazy. You can find her at the library, hurry." Breelyn felt a chill run down her spine. Despite her fears, Breelyn threw her shoes on and scrambled out the door. She was determined to find out what happened to Chloe.

The cavernous, antique looking building stood in front of Breelyn. She had never been apprehensive going into a library before. She took a deep breath to collect her nerves and crept inside. Unlike earlier, there were a few other people inside searching for books. Ms. Ignis was stationed at the front desk organizing returned items.

"Excuse me, Ms. Ignis," Breelyn began. "Have you seen another girl about my age come into the library? She's about my height and sandy blonde."

Ms. Ignis smiled, "I believe I did, child. I think she

sauntered upstairs about five minutes before you arrived."

"Thank you," Breelyn replied as she proceeded to the stairs.

"Don't mention it," Ms. Ignis smiled her crooked smile as she eyed Breelyn leaving.

Breelyn hopped up the stairs two at a time. She was tempted to call out Chloe's name, but this was a library after all. There was not a soul in sight when Breelyn reached the upper chamber. She scanned the vast expanse and witnessed row after row of bookshelves. If she weren't on such a critical mission, Breelyn would be in Heaven surrounded by this plethora of riches.

Out of the corner of her eye, Breelyn spotted someone ducking behind an aisle of books to her left. Breelyn spun in that direction. "Chloe?" she whispered as loudly as she dared. There was no response, so Breelyn picked up her pace. At the end of a section of bookshelves, she peered left but came up empty. She whirled her head to the right and caught a glimpse of the same shadowy figure disappearing into a back corner of the room.

"Chloe, is that you?" Breelyn whispered a second time as she tracked the mystery girl. She quickened her gate to a sprint, even though that was poor etiquette for a library. In a matter of seconds, she reached the end of the long aisle and followed the course Chloe had taken. Breelyn failed to locate her target, but standing before her about 40 feet away leaned against the wall was a peculiar mirror. It was unlike any mirror Breelyn had ever seen before. It was monstrous with an elaborate frame around it, and Breelyn was distracted from the search for her missing teammate.

For some reason, the bizarre antique drew her closer. She approached it warily when without warning another reflection appeared in the mirror beside her. Breelyn recognized Chloe in an instant and felt a rush of comfort sweep over her.

She wheeled around, "Hi Chloe, where were you…" Breelyn never finished her sentence because Chloe wasn't there.

"Help me," Chloe whispered. Breelyn spun back around to face the mirror. Chloe again appeared in the mirror next to Breelyn's reflection. "Help me, Breelyn." Chloe sounded as if she was in agony.

"What can I do?" Breelyn asked.

"I'm trapped. I can't get out," Chloe looked terrified.

"In the mirror, how is that possible?" Anxiety grew in Breelyn's stomach.

"I don't know. I just fell asleep last night, and when I woke up, I was here. Grab my hand. Please pull me out, Breelyn,"

Cautiously, Breelyn reached out her hand slowly, and so did Chloe. They locked eyes, and Breelyn could sense the Chloe's agony. She inched closer to Chloe's outstretched hand. Breelyn could almost grasp her. For some reason she was moving in slow motion.

"Get back!" Breelyn heard a man yell from behind her right before she could reach Chloe's fingertips. Breelyn felt herself being yanked away from the mirror.

"No! Help me! Help me! Don't leave," Chloe screamed hysterically as Breelyn was being dragged away from her.

"Let me go! Let me go! I have to save Chloe!" Breelyn shouted.

"You can't help her right now. We have to go," the man whispered as he ushered Breelyn down the stairs. Breelyn continued wriggling trying to get away.

"You have to trust me, Breelyn. We are in great danger," the man insisted.

Breelyn stopped dead in her tracks and peered into the man's eyes. He dressed in black with a white collar turned backward. He was tall and fit and appeared to be in his 30s.

"How do you know my name?" Breelyn wondered.

"I was sent to help you by a friend," the stranger replied, as they headed for the back door of the library.

"What's your name?" Breelyn questioned him.

"You can call me Brandon," he responded. "I'll explain everything to you, but first it's imperative we get out of this library. We're not safe here." They sprinted toward the back door.

Breelyn spied Ms. Ignis standing over by a table with a book in her hand. "Hello, Breelyn. Where are you going? Did you find your friend?" She smiled her crooked smile.

"Um, no, I have to go…" Breelyn stammered.

"Don't say anything more to her. Don't look back," Brandon advised. Breelyn immediately closed her mouth and turned to the exit.

"I can help you look for her," Ms. Ignis called out as Brandon pushed the door open. When Brandon and Breelyn disappeared outside, Ms. Ignis' smile vanished. If they had stayed for a few more minutes, they would have seen the tall, slender, beautiful Ms. Ignis transform into a shriveled, bespectacled old lady with her gray hair pulled up into a bun.

GATHERING THE TROOPS

THE BRILLIANT SUN BLINDED FATHER BOB as he stepped into the side alley outside the Sleepy Falls Library. Breelyn blinked and put her hand up to shield her eyes. About 20 yards away, an oversized, black van idled in the alley. Father Bob and Breelyn scuttled swiftly toward it, and the side door opened up. A lady in her mid-30s reached her hand out to aid Breelyn into the vehicle. She stood 5-foot, 9-inches tall and had an athletic build. Her shoulder length black hair framed her face perfectly.

"Hello, Breelyn. Grab my hand. It's a long way up." The dark-haired woman reached out.

Breelyn glanced at Father Bob, and he nodded. She grasped her hand and assisted Breelyn into the van.

"Brandon found another one, huh? What's your story? What did you do that got this wacko to come after you?" The woman smiled broadly, but Breelyn didn't understand why.

"Leave her alone, Samantha. She's had a rough day," Father Bob interjected.

"Relax, Brandon. I'm just joking with her. Don't worry, Breelyn. Brandon, I mean Father Bob, is a good guy. He's promised to explain why we are all here. Let me introduce you to everyone. You can sit next to me." She patted the seat beside her. Breelyn climbed into the chair and fastened her belt. Father Bob sat behind them.

"That's Grandpa Frank in the driver's seat. His grandsons, Ryan and Joe, are in the back. Ryan is the older one. Joe has blonde hair," she explained as they turned around and faced the back of the van. "Their father, Rick, is sitting next to them. That's Ashley next to Father Bob. We just picked her up from college before we grabbed you, and up front in the passenger seat is Luke. He has a little bit of an attitude, but so do I." She winked at Breelyn.

It was a lot to take in for Breelyn, and her head was spinning. "Why are we all here?" she asked.

"The good Priest hasn't told us yet," Luke chimed in sarcastically. He looked to be about Samantha's age. Luke's sandy-brown hair was cropped short. Even though he was sitting down, Breelyn could tell he was tall and built like an athlete. "He insisted we get to the library before he would tell us anything. Apparently, we needed you to join us."

"I told you," Samantha whispered to Breelyn.

"If you don't know why he wants you here, why did you agree to come with him?" Breelyn inquired.

"I can't explain it. Something told me to go with him. I felt inside that it was crucial. Hi, Breelyn. I'm Ashley." Her smile put Breelyn at ease immediately. Being separated by only nine years, Breelyn felt more comfortable with her than anyone else so far. Ashley was smaller in stature than Samantha, but beautiful, too. She had dirty blonde hair that was pulled back into a ponytail. "Don't be afraid. Everyone here is really nice, except for maybe Luke up there."

Samantha burst out laughing. Luke turned around and glared at Samantha. "So, Father, we are done with the library. Time to tell us what we are all here for," Luke spoke matter-of-factly.

"Yes, Brandon, time to come clean. What is all of this about, and how did you convince all these gullible people to get into Grandpa's van?" Samantha agreed.

"I will reveal the reasons when we get to the church," Father Bob replied cryptically as he looked out the window. Breelyn could see he was holding a rosary in his hand. It unnerved her. Why was he worried?

"Ugh." Samantha and Luke groaned. Ashley sat back

in her seat and crossed her arms. Breelyn wasn't sure what was going on, but she feared that it was something horrible. She began to regret her decision to follow Father Bob out of the library. "Sure, the mirror seemed wicked, but was this much better?"

"Why do you call him 'Brandon'?" Breelyn whispered to Samantha.

"Because that is his real name," Samantha raised her voice so everyone in the vehicle could hear. "He's my cousin. When he became a priest, he took the name Bob because that was his father's name."

Breelyn looked over at Father Bob. He never turned from the window, but he nodded affirming Samantha's story.

"That's sweet," Ashley remarked as she patted Father Bob on the shoulder.

"He died when I was very young," Father Bob explained. They sat in silence for the rest of the drive to the church. Breelyn had many questions and wasn't sure what she was doing here. Her thoughts turned to Chloe, and Breelyn wondered if Father Bob and the rest of these people could help her. After all, he had rescued her from that creepy librarian.

At long last, Grandpa turned into Father Bob's church. Brandon unlocked the hall, and they all entered the modern building. Father Bob guided them down a corridor to a small classroom. When he switched on the lights, Breelyn could see it was a classroom similar to the one she attended. She surmised it must be a fifth-grade classroom by the posters on the wall. The only differences were several religious posters and a crucifix that she would never see at her public school.

"Okay, why don't we all pull up a chair and sit down. We have a lot to discuss." Father Bob motioned to the stack in the corner. The desks had been pushed to a corner of the room leaving a big empty space in the center. The ragtag group grabbed chairs and arranged them in a circle.

"What are we here for?" Luke demanded.

"Well, about a week ago Frank and Ryan were taken from us." Father Bob motioned to Grandpa. "Now, I know this sounds crazy, but we all saw it. Somehow they were transported to another place. Imposters replaced them in this world. Rick, Joe, and I were able to rescue them." Father Bob tried to lay it out as plainly as he could. He realized how unbelievable it all sounded.

Luke looked skeptical. "What does that have to do with us?"

"Yeah, Brandon, why are we really here?" chimed in Samantha.

Father Bob was surprised they weren't questioning the story, but since they accepted it, he decided to reveal more. "I received a message advising me to bring you all together. It's the only way to prevent the mirror from harming anyone else."

"Who gave you this message?" Samantha questioned him.

Father Bob locked eyes with Samantha and hesitated for a moment. "Fred," he muttered at last as he stared at the floor.

"Are you serious?" Samantha rolled her eyes. "I thought he wasn't around anymore, Brandon. You expect all of us to stay here because Fred told you that we are necessary?"

"Who's Fred?" Ashley asked the question that was on everyone's mind.

"Fred is an imaginary friend from Brandon's childhood after his father died." Samantha slumped back disgusted.

Luke got up from his chair. "An imaginary friend told you? I've heard enough. I'm out of here. Good luck everyone." Luke sauntered toward the exit.

"He's not an imaginary friend." Father Bob's hushed tone caused them all to listen closely. "He is an angel. Yes, he was around when I was a child. His mission was to protect me, watch over me, and prepare me for this moment. Samantha, you remember what happened on that playground in fifth grade. You know Fred is real, even if you don't want to admit it."

Luke glanced over at Samantha. She flushed with embarrassment. "I don't know, Brandon. That was a long time ago."

Luke took a couple more steps toward the door to leave.

"Wait," Grandpa Frank said. "I haven't seen Fred, but I believe Father Bob. You all weren't imprisoned by a mirror last week. Two weeks ago, I would never have thought any of this was possible. However, after being transported to that cave, an angel contacting Father is par for the course."

"A mirror – you were transported using a mirror?" Breelyn blurted out. "What did it look like?"

"It was enormous, probably 10 feet by 7 feet. The bronze trim had a distressed, weathered look," said Rick, describing the mirror.

"It's the same one," whispered Breelyn.

"What's the same one?" Ashley turned to Breelyn.

"Right before you guys arrived at the library, I was searching for my friend, Chloe. The librarian told me she was upstairs, and I found her up there trapped in a mirror. It looked just like the one he described. Chloe asked me to help her. Before I could reach out to her, Father Bob showed up. She's still in danger. I have to go back there!" The thoughts raced through Breelyn's mind.

"You are lucky Father Bob showed up when he did. Otherwise, you would be trapped in that mirror with her," Grandpa Frank interjected.

"It wasn't luck, Frank. Fred told me where to go and when to be there," Father Bob corrected him.

"Okay. Let's say I believe all three of you. That still doesn't explain why I am here. I never had any mirror try to trap me," Luke uttered sarcastically as he plopped back down. "What is my connection to this?"

"I've never seen any mirror like that one either, Grandpa Frank," Ashley added.

"Yeah, Brandon, why did Fred want the three of us here," piped in Samantha.

"I don't know. Fred wouldn't tell me any more. He hinted that it was critical for us to figure out some things on our own," Father Bob answered.

"What do you think we need to figure out on our own?" questioned Rick.

"I'm guessing he wants us to figure out each of our connections to this mirror," Father Bob theorized.

"Fine, tell us more about the mirror, Frank." Luke swiveled toward Grandpa.

"Well, we were up in the attic because I was showing Ryan and Joe some pranks. We spotted the mirror under a blanket in the corner of the attic. I figured it must be my late wife's mirror, and I just didn't remember it. I was going to tell Ryan and Joe a scary story about it for laughs when we noticed inscriptions on the frame of the mirror," Grandpa recited everything from that day.

"What did the inscriptions say?" Samantha asked him.

"There were two, and they were both in Latin. The first one translated into Isaiah 5:20 out of the Bible," Father Bob explained. "It says, 'Woe to those who call good evil and evil good.' The second one seemed to be a riddle, a warning, or a spell, or something. It said, 'There is no truth. If into this mirror you wish to stare, Do not be seduced by the glare. For as a coin has two sides, so too can you into a new place ride. This doorway may seem for you a good route, but take heed when you enter in, what exits out?'"

"It seemed to activate the mirror when we read them out loud. The mirror would begin glowing green, and we heard an awful humming sound," Grandpa continued.

"Yeah, and then we were in that dark cave with all those other unfortunate people," added Ryan.

"And evil, alter egos of Grandpa and Ryan appeared." Joe shook his head.

"I didn't believe Joe at first, but the imposters gave themselves away with bizarre behavior. Fortunately, they weren't very believable," Rick assured the group.

"Horrifying," Ashley muttered.

"I remember a green light when I was trying to help Chloe," Breelyn offered.

"Interesting, but it still doesn't connect me to all of this." Luke frowned.

"Me neither," Samantha agreed.

"What else can you tell us?" Ashley asked. "What was the cave like?"

"It felt hopeless. I thought we'd never get out. I was petrified," Ryan spoke up.

"The other people trapped with us had no idea how long they had been there. It was hot, even though it was a cave-like place. We heard terrifying hissing sounds from every direction. I got the sense there were endless tunnels and dead ends, like a maze. It was utterly pitch black, except when she was there. When she showed up we could see a little bit as if candles or a campfire were illuminating the cave. Still, we all loathed when she came around," Grandpa had a pained expression.

"Who is 'she?' " Samantha asked.

"She is a teacher from the school where I was a principal. Her name is Mrs. Yorp. She was a truly malicious person who perpetrated a horrifying crime at our school. Probably served her right to be in a place like that," growled Grandpa.

"What did you say her name was?" Ashley faced Grandpa with her mouth agape.

"Mrs. Yorp. Why?" Grandpa looked quizzically at Ashley.

"I know her," Ashley replied softly.

"That's impossible. Mrs. Yorp died over 30 years ago. You have her confused with someone else," dismissed Grandpa.

"She set fire to her classroom and locked all the children inside. She killed herself and all of those sweet third graders," Ashley recounted Mrs. Yorp's crime. Now it was Grandpa's turn to be shocked.

"How did you know that?" Grandpa asked. Everyone stood transfixed on Ashley.

"My mom was a student in that class. She only survived because she was sick in the office on the day Mrs. Yorp set the blaze," Ashley explained.

"Okay, well that sheds some light on why you are here." Father Bob smiled. "Does that name ring any bells for you, Samantha or Luke?" They shook their heads.

"Are you sure it's Mrs. Yorp that you saw in the cave, Dad?" questioned Rick. "Could she have been an imposter, too, to mess with your head?"

"No. It was her," Grandpa Frank declared adamantly.

"Wait a second. Ashley, you said you know, Mrs. Yorp?" observed Samantha.

"Her mom must have told her about Mrs. Yorp," Grandpa surmised.

"That's not what she said," Samantha argued.

"Well, she did, but I know her, too. I still don't understand it, but I met her on my first day of third grade. We had just moved back to Sleepy Falls, and it was my first day at Hill Valley Elementary School. Somehow, I was in Mrs. Yorp's third-grade class, the same class as my mom. Mrs. Yorp taught me the whole day, and my mom's old friends showed me around the school. I can remember it so vividly. The next day, I went back to school, and everyone was gone — Mrs. Yorp, all my mom's friends, everyone. I had a whole new class and a new teacher.

Everyone thought I was insane," Ashley recounted the most bizarre experience of her life.

"Well, that is easy," Luke interjected. "Your mom told you about her teacher, and you had a dream that felt real." He leaned back confident he had cracked the case.

"Yes, except my mom never told me about Mrs. Yorp. When I came home from school, our house was on fire. Providentially, my mom had stayed at my grandma's house. The inferno scorched everything in our house. The only thing that survived was one photograph mocking us from the middle of the room. I recognized the lady in the picture immediately. It was Mrs. Yorp, and only then did my mom tell me the story." Everyone stared wide-eyed at Ashley. They all had goosebumps on their arms.

"Okay, now we are getting somewhere," Father Bob predicted. "What else can you tell us about that day, Frank?"

"The fire alarm went off and we evacuated the school. When we got outside, we discovered Mrs. Yorp's class was not there. I rushed back into the building along with an off-duty firefighter who happened to be in the neighborhood. We choked on the thick smoke in the hallway. I remember the awful smell and not being able to see anything. Finally, after what seemed like forever, we arrived at her room. The smoke was denser in front of her door. Captain Richard stood in front of me. He attempted to open the door, but it was locked. I remember thinking that was odd. He began prying the door open.

An immense explosion blasted us backward. The next thing I remember was waking up on a stretcher outside. Evidently, the flames had erupted when Captain Richard opened the door. He was killed instantly, while I was thrown clear. Everyone inside was already dead." Grandpa's voice trembled. Ryan and Joe hugged him.

"Wait a second," Luke sat up straight. "Captain Richard? Richard Biggio?"

"Yes. Why?" Grandpa answered slowly.

"My father died when I was two years old in a school fire. He was a firefighter named Richard Biggio." Luke looked dead serious. His sarcastic tone had vanished.

"I'm so sorry." Samantha's sarcasm evaporated as well. She draped her arm around Luke.

"What a strange coincidence," Rick mumbled.

"Illuminating," Father Bob whispered. He took notes in his book. "Did that provide any connections for you, Samantha?"

"Not for me, Brandon. Something Ashley shared jogged my memory, though. I don't know if it matters, but it seems like an odd coincidence. She met Mrs. Yorp in Sleepy Falls," Samantha began.

"Yes, that is where the fire took place. At Hill Valley Elementary School," Grandpa interrupted.

"One of my best friends growing up lived there before she moved to Springdale."

"Who?" Father Bob asked.

"Marissa." Samantha rolled her eyes.

"Yeah, I don't think that is much of a connection." Rick didn't see any significance. Samantha frowned at him.

"Fascinating," Father Bob whispered as he jotted more in his notebook.

"What is it?" Samantha straightened up in her chair.

"Fred insisted we find Marissa, too. I was going to inquire about her later, but last I heard you two weren't on speaking terms." Father Bob looked hopefully at Samantha.

"Nope, I haven't spoken to her since the mud pit." Samantha grinned while recalling that memory. "Sorry, I can't help you with that one. I don't care to see her anyway." Samantha's smile faded.

Father Bob fiddled dejectedly with his notebook. Just when they were getting somewhere they ran into another dead end. He knew Samantha to be extremely stubborn.

"My mom's name is Marissa. She was born in Sleepy Falls and later grew up in Springdale," Breelyn blurted out.

Everyone in the group whirled to face the 10-year-old.

"How old is your mom?" Samantha questioned her.

"She just turned 36 on the third," Breelyn replied.

"That's her," Samantha muttered to Father Bob with a grimace.

"Are you sure?" Father Bob questioned his cousin.

"Yes, definitely. She is the same age as me, and I remember her birthday," Samantha affirmed.

"You know my mom?" Breelyn inquired.

"Yes, sweetheart. We were friends in elementary school," Samantha responded.

"Cool. What happened after that? Did you move?" Breelyn wondered.

Father Bob and Samantha exchanged glances. "We have no time to waste. Who knows what other damage Mrs. Yorp may be doing right now? Can you take us to your house, Breelyn, so that we can speak to your mother?" Father Bob queried.

"Sure. My mom will be off work soon. I'm sure she will be excited to see you, Samantha," exclaimed Breelyn.

Samantha shot a sideways look at Father Bob, but he just nodded. Father Bob's band got up from their chairs, and they relocated to Grandpa's van. Samantha and Father Bob fretted over what they would say to Marissa when arriving at Breelyn's house. Samantha hadn't seen her in 18 years and hadn't talked to her in over 20 years. Father Bob was optimistic she had changed. According to Fred, Marissa was part of the solution to this whole puzzle.

"Breelyn, just you and I will go in to see your mother," Father Bob informed her.

"You're not coming in, Samantha?" Breelyn asked.

"No, honey, I think it's best if I stay here." Samantha attempted to elude divulging any of their past.

The duo hopped out of the vehicle and began to hike up the driveway to the front door. "Why isn't Samantha coming with us?" Breelyn questioned Father Bob.

"Have you ever had a falling out with a friend?" Father Bob began.

"I guess so. One of my best friends from last year hates my guts this year. I don't even know what I did. Girls can be ruthless sometimes," Breelyn confided in Father Bob.

Father Bob chuckled. "So you understand. That's why it's probably best if we just talk to your mother and not tell her Samantha is here until she needs to know."

"I know my mom has some issues and can rub people the wrong way, but she has a good heart. I've seen it," Breelyn said defensively.

"I believe you, Breelyn. Fred wouldn't have sent us here if she didn't," Father Bob assured her. Breelyn cracked a smile and pulled out her key to let them into the house.

"Is that you, Breelyn?" Marissa yelled from the kitchen as she jogged toward the front door. "Where were you? I was worried. You didn't even leave a note! Who is this?"

"I'm sorry, Mom. I was at the library. It's a long story. This is Father Bob. He will explain everything." Breelyn answered her mom hurriedly so she wouldn't flip out.

"Hi, Bob — would you like to tell me what is going on here?" Marissa spoke curtly.

"Yes, ma'am. Can we sit down first?" Father Bob answered.

Marissa rolled her eyes. "Sure. There is a couch right there." She pointed to the front room. The three of them sat down on the worn, grey sofa. "Okay, so why was my daughter at the library? Why is she coming back with you?" Marissa interrogated bluntly.

"I saw Breelyn searching for her friend at the library. There was a strange person in the building who creeped Breelyn out. She was afraid he was going to follow her outside, so we thought I should give her a ride home." Father Bob revealed a partial truth.

Marissa looked skeptical, but Father Bob turned the tables. "Have you ever had any odd incidents with an antique mirror?" Marissa's reaction let him know she had not.

"Why don't you tell me what this is really about?" Marissa was not a fool.

"Okay Mom. We are going to tell you, but you have to believe us, no matter how crazy it sounds," Breelyn interjected.

Marissa raised an eyebrow at her daughter. "Go for it."

"One of my friends from my soccer team disappeared. No one else remembers her. I found a note telling me she was at the library. When I arrived, the librarian told me she was upstairs. I searched for Chloe and discovered she was trapped in this eerie mirror. I tried to help her, but Father Bob pulled me out of there. That thing is dangerous, and he saved me." Breelyn endeavored to summarize the day's events.

Marissa again looked incredulous, but she wanted to hear more. "How did you know it was dangerous?"

"A similar mirror sucked two parishioners of mine into it, and we had to rescue them. I've been studying the relic, and an angel visited me to give me guidance. He told me I should gather certain people to prevent this mirror from causing any more havoc. One of the names given to me was Breelyn's. He told me where she was, and that she was in trouble. The angel also gave me your name." Marissa's expression changed slightly as Father Bob gave her more details. Maybe she was considering the possibility that there was some truth to the story.

"I don't know why he would give you my name. I've never seen a mirror like the one you described," she stated.

"Okay, well what about Sleepy Falls? Did you grow up there?" Father Bob recalled that Sleepy Falls had jogged Samantha's memory.

Marissa's expression changed again. "I haven't thought about that town in a long time. I lived there until I was 4. Sorry, I'm sure that doesn't help."

Father Bob pulled out his notebook and jotted the information down.

"You know, while we have been sitting here talking, I can't get over the feeling that I know you from somewhere. Have we met before?" Marissa asked.

"Have you ever heard of a Mrs. Yorp?" Father Bob was running out of time. He worried Marissa would figure out how she knew him and would stop cooperating.

"Why would you ask that?" Marissa jolted back in her chair. Breelyn saw a look come over her Mom's face she hadn't seen since her father walked out on them. Tears welled up in her eyes. "Does this have some connection to that monster?"

"We believe it does," Father Bob replied. "I'm sorry if this is painful, but can you tell me how you know her?"

"When we lived in Sleepy Falls, I was 4. My big sister Caitlin was 9. I looked up to her so much. I loved Caitlin and wanted to be just like her. I would follow her around everywhere, dress up like her, and imitate her. Gosh, I must have been so annoying. Caitlin always let me play with her friends. She always included me, you know. She just had a heart of gold. Everyone loved her…" Marissa's voice trailed off. She was lost deep in thought.

After a moment she continued, "One day we got a call. I was playing with my dolls waiting for Caitlin to come home. I can still picture my mom screaming and crying hysterically. There had been a fire at the school.

Mrs. Yorp locked the door and set fire to her classroom. Caitlin was…" Marissa's voice cracked, and tears were streaming down her face. "I'm sorry. After that, nothing was the same. My parents grew distant. I don't think they knew how to deal with it. They became irritated easily and lost their tempers a lot. We stopped going to church. We moved from Sleepy Falls the next year, but it didn't help. The truth is, our family never recovered. I began acting like such a jerk. I didn't know how to be kind to people because I was filled with rage. Caitlin would be so ashamed of who I am…" Marissa put her head in her hands and couldn't go on.

Father Bob got up and put his hand around Marissa's shoulder. "I'm sorry Marissa. I can't imagine what it must have been like to lose a sister. Thank you for sharing with us. Fred never told me about this."

Marissa paused and looked up at Father Bob with tears in her eyes. She discreetly wiped her eyes with the back of her hand. "Fred? Wait a second. I know why I recognize you. You're Samantha's cousin, Brandon. You had an imaginary friend named Fred."

Father Bob grinned. "You're right, except the imaginary part. I always told everyone he was real. Recently, he reappeared and revealed to me that he is an angel."

"And he told you about Mrs. Yorp, and sent you to see me?" Marissa connected the dots.

"Yes, pretty much," Father Bob replied.

"Okay, so what's your proposal?"

"We would appreciate it if you accompany us, so we can try to solve this riddle."

Marissa collected her purse and keys and followed them out the door. "I should probably let you know that Samantha is with us," Father Bob apprised Marissa.

"Great," Marissa mumbled.

"Hello everyone, this is Breelyn's mom, Marissa," Father Bob introduced her as they climbed into the vehicle. The group greeted her warmly, other than Samantha. She had moved to the far back seat and gazed out the window.

"Hello, Samantha." Marissa took a shot at breaking the ice.

"Hi. Thanks for coming," Samantha muttered.

"I believe Marissa shed some more light on our situation. Her sister was in Mrs. Yorp's class the year of the fire," he said grimly. "That's why her family moved to Springdale."

There was an audible gasp in the backseat. Ashley covered her mouth with her hand in shock. Samantha's eyes began to water. "I'm so sorry, Marissa. I had no idea your sister died in a fire. I can't imagine what it must have been like."

"Thank you, Sam. I'm so sorry for everything I did to you growing up. I was immature, mean, and angry. I wish I could take it all back," Marissa sobbed.

"I forgive you. I'm sorry I wasn't able to help you at the time." Samantha and Marissa hugged. Father Bob was relieved by the unexpected reconciliation.

"That's great. I'm happy for you two. Now, what are we supposed to do?" Luke steered the conversation back to business.

"It's obvious that Mrs. Yorp is behind all of this. She killed your father, Marissa's sister, tried to kill Ashley and her mother, and tried to trap Ryan and Frank," Father Bob explained. "I believe Fred is asking us to put a stop to Mrs. Yorp's reign of terror."

"Right, I agree, Father. I believe the mirror is the source of her power. I think it is how she moves around. If we destroy the mirror, we destroy her," Grandpa theorized. "I've been waiting 30 years to settle a score. Let's not waste any time."

"Come on, do you all really believe this? That woman has been dead for 30 years." Luke rolled his eyes. "I haven't seen the mirror or this dead lady. It sounds to me like you are all crazy. I've heard about enough of this nonsense. It was nice meeting everyone. Now please take me back to the church so I can get my car."

"Luke, maybe this will help you," Joe's little voice from the back of the van called out. "It's not what happens to you in life, but how you react to it. Remember, I am always watching over you, and I'm proud of you."

"Where did you hear that?" Luke froze.

"I found it sitting back here. It said, 'To Luke' on it," Joe replied.

"That's not funny," Luke shook his head sternly.

"Here it is. See for yourself." Joe passed the paper forward. Luke scanned it, and then pulled his wallet out. He reached inside and pulled out a folded up photo.

"I haven't looked at this since college," Luke began. "It's a note my dad wrote to me when I was 12 years old."

"I thought your dad died when you were two?" Rick asked.

"That's right," agreed Ryan.

"He did, but when I was 12, a new guy showed up to play for our baseball team. He played the whole season for us, and we became great friends. After the championship game, he disappeared into the woods, so I went looking for him. I couldn't find him, but I did come across a headstone and this photograph." Luke turned the folded up picture toward everyone. "The photo was of the player who disappeared. When I showed it to my mom, she told me it was actually a picture of my dad when he was my age. On the back, was the same message that you just read."

"Let me see that," Father Bob asked as Luke handed him the photograph. He examined the message on the back alongside the note Joe had pulled out of his Bible. "The handwriting looks identical. See for yourself." He handed them back to Luke.

Luke studied the two messages. He nodded.

"What does it mean?" Rick asked.

"It means we aren't as crazy as Luke thought," Father Bob grinned at Luke.

Luke smirked. "Okay. Maybe I'm insane too."

"Excellent!" Grandpa pumped his fist in the driver's seat. "Let's head to Father Bob's house and destroy the mirror and Mrs. Yorp once and for all." The crew let out a triumphant yell, and Grandpa floored it. In no time, they were back in the church parking lot and piling out of the van.

"Okay, I have the mirror in the back bedroom for safekeeping," Father Bob explained as they walked through the front door. "We don't know what to expect from this mirror, so I think it's best if Frank, Rick, Luke, and I go in first to check it out."

"Don't be ridiculous. I'm going in there. You might need me, Brandon," Samantha elbowed past him.

"I know there is no point trying to talk you out of anything. Marissa and Ashley, would you mind watching the children?" Father Bob relented.

"Sure," they said in unison.

"Thank you," Father Bob replied as the five of them disappeared into the back bedroom. A moment later they returned into the living room.

"I knew you were all crazy," Luke exclaimed. "This has been a waste of time."

Ashley looked confused. "What happened?" she asked.

"There is nothing in that bedroom," Luke spat out disgustedly.

"I'm telling you, it was there when I left this morning," Father Bob insisted.

"Sure it was. I'm sure that dead lady Mrs. Yorp climbed out of her grave and stole it." Luke pretended to be a zombie.

"I believe you, Father," Breelyn spoke up.

"Of course you do – you're eight," Luke shot back.

"I'm 10," Breelyn corrected him with a serious look on her face. "And I saw the mirror in the library. I know it exists. Think about everything that has happened to all of us. Does a mirror disappearing really seem far-fetched?"

"She's got you there, champ," Samantha playfully punched Luke in the shoulder.

"We saw the mirror, too, and we know Father Bob brought it here," Grandpa reminded Luke. "I say we head to the library before that one disappears, too."

"Good idea, Grandpa," Ryan agreed.

"Yes, the library is definitely the next place we should search," Rick concurred.

"Okay, fine. What's one more wild goose chase," Luke relented.

"So Breelyn, what do you like to do?" Ashley always

wanted to get to know people better. She figured it would pass the time on the ride to the library.

"Well, I love to read, and play soccer," Breelyn replied.

Ashley's eyes lit up. "No way, I play soccer in college! What position are you?"

"I'm a forward," Breelyn answered. "What about you?"

"I play attacking center mid. I bet you score a ton of goals." She winked at Breelyn.

"I guess. I'm averaging almost two goals a game in the gold division right now. I have plenty of things to improve on, though. I hope one day I can play in college like you! I bet you're amazing!" Breelyn dreamed of playing in college, and now she was hanging out with a college player.

"I'm okay," Ashley replied modestly. "We had a pretty good season. We made it to the Final Four. Maybe someday we can play on the national team together. I can always use a good forward to receive my passes."

"That would be great! It sure would be fun! Tell me about your season. What's playing in college like?" Breelyn wanted details. The two girls continued talking soccer on the way to the library. Time flew by, and before they knew it, Grandpa was parking.

"Okay, Breelyn, you come in with us this time. You know the library better than anyone. Grandpa will wait in the car with the rest of you. If we aren't back in 10 minutes, go get help." Father Bob laid out the plan. He worried they might be walking into an ambush.

"Forget that. I'm coming in after you. I'm not letting Yorp win this time." Grandpa gritted his teeth.

"Don't worry. She won't." Luke clenched his jaw and glared at the library.

The team of five ventured into the library to search for the evil antique. Breelyn felt a sense of relief when she saw Ms. Brent, her favorite librarian, behind the desk this time. She waved to her as they climbed upstairs to the top floor.

"Try to avoid looking directly into the mirror, and whatever you do, don't read the inscriptions," Father Bob warned them as he pulled out items from the bag he was carrying. He handed a large crowbar to Samantha and baseball bats for Luke and himself. He also had a baseball and a brick. "Just in case we can't get close enough to destroy the mirror. I thought a hand grenade might be overkill," he joked.

When they reached the top of the stairs, Breelyn pointed to the left. "The mirror is over there." Father Bob led the way. Rick, Samantha, and Luke were right behind him, and Breelyn brought up the rear.

"It's down that row of bookshelves," Breelyn insisted. The group crept closer to the corner Breelyn indicated. The second floor of the library was deadly silent, and the dim lights above flickered. Breelyn reached out for Samantha and grasped her hand.

Five more steps and Father Bob reached the end of the aisle. He backed up against the books, and slowly peered around the corner. Rick and Luke stood next to him and watched Father Bob for direction. Samantha and Breelyn held their breath. Father Bob straightened up and stepped out into the open.

"Are you sure it was this corner?" he asked Breelyn. Everyone followed him out into the open and saw why his body language had changed. Another large cabinet full of books sat in the corner.

"I'm positive. It was right in front of that bookcase," Breelyn replied adamantly.

"Okay, well let's investigate the rest of this floor to make sure someone didn't move it," Father Bob suggested.

The group searched every inch of the top floor of the library and even scanned the first floor, but they found no sign of the mirror.

"I don't understand why the mirrors are disappearing," Father Bob thought out loud. Samantha, Luke, and Rick stood glumly next to him.

"What's the next move?" Rick whispered.

"Let's go to the van and figure it out," Samantha suggested. The grownups didn't notice Breelyn walk over to Ms. Brent, while they conversed. After a few moments,

Breelyn returned to the group.

"Excuse me," she began politely. The adults stopped their conversation and looked down at the 10-year-old. "I know what happened to the mirror. Some movers came and got it a couple of hours ago. Ms. Brent overheard them saying they were taking it to the County Office of Education."

"Well I guess we are taking another road trip," Father Bob nodded at Luke.

"They took it to the Office of Education," Samantha updated the rest of the group as they climbed into the van.

"Figures Mrs. Yorp would take them there," Grandpa muttered.

"What do you mean?" Ashley asked.

"She was very involved in union activism and spent so much time at the Office of Education for the latest, 'cutting-edge' training. Other teachers used to joke that she was off campus more than she was teaching," Grandpa recalled. He pushed his foot down on the gas pedal, and they sped away from the library. The showdown with Mrs. Yorp and the mirror was imminent.

GRANDMASTER

"SHE'S LOSING IT. I THINK THE OLD WOMAN is getting desperate," whispered a tall disfigured man to his stout companion.

"What do you mean?" the corpulent, black-haired man replied.

"They are getting closer. Yorp keeps moving the mirrors. She must feel they are in danger," the first one replied. The goatee on his face masked his worry.

"I agree, Haman. She should never have called us back." The girthy cohort's brow furrowed with anger. "We had the situation under control. She made a grave mistake."

"Exactly, Herod, and now they have us on the run. The master will not be pleased with her. We need to make sure he knows we didn't support her decision." Haman plotted their damage control.

A sudden flicker of flames illuminated the dark cave, and the two associates quickly halted their discussion. The hissing sounds of snakes interrupted the quiet.

"Don't stop grumbling on my account." The familiar cackle sent shivers up Haman and Herod's backs.

"We weren't grumbling, your eminence." Haman attempted to backtrack.

"Silence! Your excuses insult me. I find your lack of faith irritating, and so does the master." The evil harridan seemed to look right through her two henchmen. "What is it that has shaken your trust? And don't lie to me again."

"Why did you bring us back here? We were in a position to cause chaos. Now, we are retreating, and they are getting close to the mirror," Herod spat out the accusations without any tact. Haman cowered in anticipation of recompense.

Mrs. Yorp glared at them both with a steely gaze. They could see her black eyes reflect the flames all around them. Her eyes seemed to burn with the fiery blaze. They awaited her violent temper. Slowly a smirk appeared on her face. She turned and motioned to a thigh-high boulder behind them.

"Are you familiar with this game?" she pointed to the game board sitting atop the boulder. They nodded. "Chess is one of my favorite games. It is so applicable to every phase of life. I used to teach it to all my students. I studied it for many years and perfected my craft as a Grandmaster."

Haman and Herod nodded and exchanged glances. They figured the old woman must really be losing her mind. Mrs. Yorp sat down at the chessboard and tapped it to gain their attention once more.

"The thing about chess is the foresight and the planning that it takes to be a good player." She began shuffling pieces around on the board. "There are a million different combinations of moves that one can make. These scenarios must be seen. They must be anticipated. You must think through what you can do. What your opponent may do, how they will react to your play, gambits to gain an advantage. It's elegant."

Mrs. Yorp continued simulating a chess match. "You see, the novice player often becomes preoccupied with capturing his opponent's pieces. He becomes focused on the immediate move. He captures a pawn, or a knight, or a rook, and thinks it is a victory." Mrs. Yorp began removing captured pieces from the board. "All the while, little by little, he is actually losing the match. However, the Grandmaster plans ahead. She always has her mind on how to win the war, not a battle. The ultimate outcome of the match is foremost in her thoughts. She sees 10 moves ahead. She lays a trap for her opponent. The Grandmaster is willing to sacrifice pawns for her opponent's queen." Mrs. Yorp nodded at Haman and Herod.

"In the end, it doesn't matter how many pawns she sacrifices. All that matters is capturing the king. Do you understand?" Haman and Herod nodded even though they had puzzled expressions.

"I have laid a trap for them. They only see the next move, while my trap is 10 moves down the line. My pawns may have been lost, but other pieces have been hidden on the board, and they are key to our ultimate victory." The old Chess Grandmaster brought an extra queen off from the side of the board that Haman hadn't seen before.

"Yes, but why not trap them in the mirror? We had them." Herod still was caught up in the lost opportunity.

"I just can't spell it out for some people. Winning a battle is not the goal. Winning the war is our focus. Capturing a piece or two is not victory." Two of Mrs. Yorp's pets slithered across her feet, and her wrinkled face took on an evil smile.

"What is victory, then?" Haman wondered.

"Indeed. I have taken inspiration from my second favorite story, The Trojan Wars. Beware the Trojan Horse," she cackled mysteriously.

"I don't understand." Mrs. Yorp's cryptic response confused Herod.

"Our game is total devastation and tragedy so that the ripples destroy everyone around. Most people react to a tragic loss by losing their hope and faith. Not only do we ruin one life, but the domino effect on everyone else connected to that life will be marvelous. That is how you achieve total victory." Mrs. Yorp laid out her plans like an evil general.

On the gameboard, she slid her second queen into position. "Checkmate," she whispered. The flames in the cave mysteriously extinguished themselves, and Mrs. Yorp vanished.

Grandpa hung a left and neared the entrance to the south freeway. The County Office of Education would be another 15 miles up the highway. In the back of the vehicle, Ryan and Joe sat alone worried about the outcome of the confrontation.

"Something is wrong, Joe. Why do the mirrors keep disappearing?" Ryan questioned his brother.

"I'm telling you, she must have a spy. That is not our Dad. I don't trust him," Joe insisted.

"Not this again. Dad's totally normal. Don't you think Mom would have noticed if something was different about him?" Ryan thought logically.

Joe had to admit that he hadn't seen any signs of Dad being an imposter at home. He hadn't been acting peculiar. Unquestionably, Rick hadn't outwardly sabotaged their mission so far. Still, Joe remained convinced the man in the van was not his real dad. Joe required evidence to prove beyond a shadow of a doubt that he was correct. Up front, Rick discussed strategy with the other adults much to Joe's chagrin.

"It's worth a try. That plan might work," Grandpa mumbled. "First, we need to get gas though," he said after glancing down at the display. The gauge showed they had less than a quarter tank left. The gas station was a block before the freeway entrance, and Frank pulled in earnestly. There was no time to waste, if they wanted to stop Mrs. Yorp. Everyone except Father Bob and Joe piled out of the car and headed into the convenience store to load up on snacks and use the restroom.

"Can I talk to you for a minute, Father?" Joe's little voice broke the silence in the van while Grandpa filled up the tank.

"Sure, Joe, what's on your mind?" Father Bob's warm smile emboldened Joe.

"I think we have a problem, Father. I believe one of us is not who they claim to be. I'm afraid the traitor is spying for Mrs. Yorp, and that is why she is a step ahead of us. I have an idea, though." Father Bob listened intently to Joe. Something was telling him to trust the 8-year-old. After Joe had laid out his plan, Grandpa climbed into the van, and the others returned from the store.

"Frank, let's stop by the church before we head to the

school. I have some things I need to pick up."

"Sure, no problem, Father," Grandpa replied from the driver's seat. He turned down the road toward St. James. When they arrived, Father Bob made an announcement to the group.

"I think we should all go into the church and say a little prayer to help with our mission. It won't hurt our cause, that's for sure," Father Bob explained. Marissa and Luke rolled their eyes, but the group piled out of Grandpa's vehicle and honored the priest's request. Inside, Father Bob led them in a short prayer asking for God's guidance and protection. When he concluded, Father Bob pulled out a small glass jar.

"I'm going to say a little blessing over each of you," he explained as he dipped his hand in the Holy Water. Frank took his turn first, and Father Bob made the sign of the cross with the Holy Water on Frank's head as he prayed. Luke and Samantha were blessed by Father Bob next, and then he moved over to Rick.

"Bow your head, Rick," Father Bob instructed.

Rick took a step back from Father Bob and the Holy Water. "No, thank you, Father," he mumbled. Joe looked up at his father with concern.

"This is vital, Rick. We need all the protection we can get," Father Bob explained.

"I don't need it, you can bless the others, Father." Rick dug in his heels.

"Okay, suit yourself," Father Bob relented. He turned toward Ashley, but at the last second wheeled around and sprinkled some Holy Water onto Rick.

"Tsssssst," an audible burning sound filled the church. "Ahhh!" Rick growled in pain. Father Bob could see his face had started to melt where the Holy Water had landed, revealing a pock-marked, grey creature underneath. "You shouldn't have done that, priest," the beast hissed as it scampered out of the church.

Everyone watched in stunned horror, not believing what they were seeing.

"You were right, Joe," Father Bob whispered as he put his arm around him.

"What happened to Dad?" Joe asked. "Where is he?"

"It must have happened back in the attic," Father Bob hypothesized. "I'm sorry, Joe. I told your dad to look away. He threw the blanket on me, pushed me out of the way and took my place. He's a hero." Father Bob looked devastated. "Mrs. Yorp must have switched him with that creature, and we didn't realize it."

"I noticed something was wrong when he threw the keys to Grandpa with the wrong hand," Joe recalled.

"Now he's gone for good," Ryan hung his head. Everyone's face fell, and their hearts were moved with pity for the boys.

"Wait a second," Father Bob perked up a little. "Remember when imposter Grandpa told us about the hidden part of the inscription that is used to reverse the mirror?"

Joe nodded. "What about it?"

"I recognized it from John 1:5. It means the light shines in the darkness, and the darkness has not overcome it."

"So what are you saying, Father?" Grandpa asked.

"I believe we can still save Rick. The light is more powerful than the darkness. We need to get back to those mirrors though." Father Bob remained steadfast.

"Let's do it," Luke gritted his teeth. The group resolutely adjourned to the van while Father Bob locked up the church. When he had finished, he joined them, and they resumed their trek to the County Office of Education.

In the backseat, Joe still clutched his father's Bible under his arm. It reminded him of his dad, and he needed the comfort. He glanced down and noticed a piece of paper protruding near the back of the Bible. Joe cracked open the Bible and pulled out a folded up piece of paper. He opened the letter and began to read:

Joe,

If you are reading this, then I am no longer with you. I'm sorry, son. I did what I believe God asked me to do in the attic. I love you, Mom, and Ryan more than anything in this world. I would do anything for you three, including laying down my life. I think Father Bob is the key to this. I'm not sure what his role is going to be, but I know God has a unique need for him if we are to stop this evil. I am prepared to do whatever I have to do to get Ryan and Grandpa back. Just remember to stick together with your brother and Mom. Always follow God. I love you, Joe. Give your brother a hug and Mom a kiss for me.

Love you,

Dad

Joe was fighting back the tears as he read the note. After he reread the letter, Joe looked down at the Bible. His father had circled the passage of John 15:13. It read:

"No one has greater love than this, to lay down one's life for one's friends."

10

GOOD VS EVIL

"EXCUSE ME. THERE WAS AN OVERSIZED mirror delivered here today. We have reason to believe the wrong one got sent by mistake. Can we inspect it?" Samantha asked, posing as a furniture saleswoman. "We hate for our customers to be unhappy with their purchases."

The middle-aged receptionist at the desk peered up from his work and frowned at them. They could see his name tag read, 'Herbert.' "I did see a box come in earlier. A shorter lady and two men took it upstairs. Let me call up and see if they don't mind you taking a look." Luke and Samantha exchanged glances. They couldn't risk tipping off Mrs. Yorp. Samantha nodded at Frank, activating their contingency plan.

"We insist," Luke growled in his best tough-guy voice. He snatched the phone away from the shocked clerk.

"Hey, what do you think you're doing?" Herbert shrieked while searching under his desk for the panic button.

"Ah, ah, ah," Luke said wagging his finger at him, "hands where I can see them."

Frank and Father Bob quickly came in from around the corner and yanked Herbert back from the desk in his roller chair. Father Bob produced a roll of gorilla tape from his jacket and clamped a piece over Herbert's mouth. They proceeded to bind his hands together at the wrist and tape his legs to the chair. Meanwhile, Samantha slyly inspected the open rooms down the hallway.

"Here, this one is good," she cried out. Frank and Father Bob rolled Herbert into the room. Samantha closed the door, locking him inside.

"Okay, we won't have much time. Let's head upstairs," Father Bob whispered.

"Yes, but what floor?" Grandpa asked. "There are four floors."

"Let me check." Samantha walked over to Herbert's desk. "Here is a delivery manifest. It looks like the delivery went to room 402, on the top floor."

"Good work, Samantha." Father Bob praised her as they made a beeline for the elevator. "Be ready. I'm sure

Yorp will be up there with the mirror. With any luck, we can catch her by surprise."

The elevator doors opened, and Luke stepped out onto the fourth level. He glanced up and down the hallway and then motioned for the others to follow him into the empty corridor.

"Room 402 is this way," Samantha motioned to the left. As they walked down a long hallway, they heard footsteps approaching from around the corner, and froze in their tracks. Two men emerged from the adjoining hall. The first gentleman appeared to be about Grandpa's age, had grey hair, and wore a sharp suit. The second man towered over everyone in the hallway. He was around 30 years old. His hulking, 6-foot, 9-inch frame filled out his suit completely. Luke could tell he was no stranger to the weight room. The two men were speaking to each other in low tones and nodded as they passed Grandpa, Samantha, Luke, and Father Bob in the corridor. Suddenly, they paused, and the older gentleman looked back at them.

"Frank? How are you doing?" he asked warmly.

"Hi Herm. I'm well. How are you?" Grandpa replied.

"Fine, fine. It's been a long time. It's good to see you. What are you doing here?" Herm struck Luke as overly friendly. Samantha could tell the expression plastered on his face was phony. The one you might see from a politician or a used car salesman.

"Oh, just coming by to see some old friends. My nephew and niece, and her husband are thinking of moving here. They wanted to check out the school districts, so I'm giving them a grand tour," lied Grandpa.

"Wonderful. Good idea, it's a great school district." Herm nodded to Samantha, Luke, and Father Bob. "I'm the superintendent of the schools. This is my associate Hal Goit." He turned to the mountain of a man on his left. "He would be glad to show you around."

"Oh, that won't be necessary. We can manage," Grandpa assured him.

"Nonsense, I insist." Herm's smile lost some of its friendliness.

"Okay. Thank you." Grandpa relented. Herm nodded toward Hal who gestured around the corner and turned to lead the way. Glumly, the four followed Hal and silently wondered how they would slip away to find the mirror.

Hal stopped in front of room 405. The mirror was only three doors away, but might as well have been 300 miles away.

"Why don't we start with this room? It's our board room. You can see a model of the city. It will show you where all of the schools are located," Hal explained in a deep voice that matched his muscular frame perfectly. Father Bob and Samantha walked into the room first, followed by Frank, and then Luke. In the back, they could see the podium for the board members. Off to the side, they saw a model of the city.

"Click," Luke heard the door close behind him. He turned around to see Hal standing by the door.

"Mrs. Yorp says, 'Hello,'" Hal sneered as a colossal right hand caromed off Luke's jaw. Luke staggered back stunned. His knees buckled, and he had to put his hand down on the floor to brace his fall. His vision was blurry, and the room seemed to be spinning. Hal kicked Luke in the gut and then turned his attention to Father Bob who was throwing a punch towards Hal's jaw. A massive hand swallowed up Father Bob's fist in midair.

"Ha, ha, ha," bellowed the giant. "You will have to do better than that, priest!" His beefy mitts enveloped Father Bob's neck and began choking him. Father Bob grasped at Hal's hands, desperately trying to pry them off of his throat. Father Bob's eyes began to tear up, and the room started going black. At the last instant before passing out, he felt Hal's gargantuan paws loosen their grip. Grandpa had chop blocked Hal's knee causing it to buckle. The giant was now down on one knee and turned his attention toward Grandpa. He reached up in an effort to seize him, but Grandpa backed away.

Samantha delivered a kick to the back of Hal's head, causing him to be dazed momentarily. He whirled around to see who had kicked him, but Grandpa booted him in the gut. Luke had somewhat recovered from the first punch by now. He grabbed a chair from the room and struck Herm's associate over the head. Hal's eyes rolled into the back of his head. He collapsed face first onto the floor like a giant oak tree.

Grandpa scrambled over to check on Father Bob who was attempting to catch his breath.

"Are you okay, Luke?" Samantha asked concerned.

"Yeah, I'm fine. That overgrown punk can't keep me down," Luke assured her. His jaw was sore, and he had a massive headache, but Luke was coherent.

Back in the van, Ryan and Joe were worried and impatient.

"We need to do something, Joe," Ryan whispered to his brother. "They have been gone too long."

"I know. What if they are in trouble?" Joe agreed.

"We need to get in there," Ryan urged his brother. In the back seat, Marissa, Ashley, and Breelyn were talking amongst themselves. Stealthily, Ryan and Joe slipped out of the side door and left it slightly ajar to avoid alerting the girls. They had sprinted the 50 yards to the front of the office building by the time Marissa noticed they were missing.

"Did Ryan and Joe leave?" she asked Ashley as she scanned the front of the van. "Ugh, boys," she grumbled. "We better go save them. Grandpa is going to be furious if anything happens to them. Come on, girls." Marissa,

Ashley, and Breelyn followed the boys into the building.

"Are you sure it's Room 402, Ryan?" Joe asked his brother during the elevator ride.

"Yes, it was right there on the reception desk. It showed a delivery to this room today. It has to be it," Ryan informed his brother.

"Let's get over to Room 402 before anyone else comes looking for Hal," Father Bob implored the group moments after they had tied up the giant. They nodded, and Grandpa peered outside the boardroom. The hallway was abandoned, so they proceeded to their left until they reached Room 402. Father Bob handed out weapons and slowly turned the knob. The door opened, and they ventured inside the pitch-black room. Samantha felt around for the light switch on the wall but couldn't find one.

"Maybe we are in the wrong room," she whispered.

"No, you are in the right room," an evil voice laughed. A dim light popped on in the center of the room, illuminating the two mirrors. Immediately, the dreadful green glow of the mirrors lit the place up further. Mrs. Yorp stepped out of the mirror on the left and into their presence.

"Hello, Frank. Nice to see you again," she cackled. "I see you brought the priest and some friends with you," she hissed in Father Bob's direction. "Well, I brought some friends of my own." Mrs. Yorp laughed, and three figures stepped out of the shadows. Two of them were hulking men dressed in black suits. Fortunately, they weren't as gigantic as Hal. One stood only a couple inches shorter than Hal. The other was about Luke's height, but very rotund. Father Bob read the name tag lapels on the two men. Haman and Herod were printed neatly on them. He glanced over to see that the third figure was a woman named Delilah.

"We are planning a party. Why don't you join us?" Mrs. Yorp's raspy voice signaled her thugs. Haman and Herod made a beeline for Grandpa and grabbed him on either side. They dragged him toward the mirror. Delilah overpowered Samantha and pulled her by the hair in the same direction.

Mrs. Yorp produced a cane from behind the mirror and threw it down into the room. Instantly, it transformed into a 10-foot snake. Mrs. Yorp's pet sprang toward Father Bob and wrapped around his wrists tightly. Father Bob dropped the baseball bat that he had been holding.

"What do you want, Yorp? Is it because I didn't die in the fire? Let the rest of these people go," yelled Grandpa.

"Oh, it is much bigger than you, Frank. I have plans for all of them. You'll see." Her laugh creeped Samantha out. The handle of Room 402 turned, opening the brown door. Ryan and Joe stepped inside and their eyes adjusted to the dim green light in time to see their friends in peril.

"Luke, do something," Samantha pleaded. Luke sprang into action. He bolted for Father Bob and pulled the baseball out of Father Bob's pocket. Luke hoped his right arm still had some life left. His cannon circled back and whipped forward, exploding the white spheroid out of his hand. Luke knew it was a bullseye as soon as he let it go. He watched as it headed toward the dead center of the glowing green mirror.

"Not today, Yorp," he shouted as he waited for the beautiful sound of breaking glass. It never came. Luke's eyes widened in surprise as the ball changed direction about a foot in front of the mirror. It rocketed off to the side and rattled off the wall.

"Yes, it will be today, and you're joining us," she gurgled as she threw down another cane into the middle of the room. Luke knew what to expect, however. He deftly dodged the snake with the same move he used to employ when sliding into second base. Luke rolled over near the Louisville Slugger that Father Bob had dropped.

"No, thank you. I hate parties," Luke quipped as he popped up and sprinted for Mrs. Yorp's evil portals. The snake continued its pursuit.

"Smash the mirror, Luke!" Frank yelled as he attempted to hold off Mrs. Yorp's henchmen.

Luke cocked the bat back, but before he could swing, the snake wrapped itself around his wrist. Haman and Herod wriggled away from Frank and grabbed Luke, dislodging the bat from his hands.

"We need to help Grandpa," Joe pleaded with Ryan as they hid in the corner.

"I know, but how?" Ryan asked.

"Let's get the bat for him, and then distract the others so he can smash the mirror." Joe devised a plan.

"Okay, let's do it, brother," Ryan affirmed.

"Remember what Dad always told us, 'If you boys stick together, work hard and help each other…'" Joe waited for his brother to finish the familiar mantra.

Ryan grinned, "'then we will always win.' Don't worry, Joe, I know what to do." Ryan sprinted over to where the Louisville Slugger had rolled. He deftly retrieved it and locked eyes with Grandpa. "Heads up, Grandpa," Ryan called out as he tossed the baseball bat to Frank. Grandpa speared it with one hand and slowly fixed his gaze on his target. The grin on his face and the fire in his eyes betrayed the determination coursing through his veins. He would defeat Mrs. Yorp if it was the last thing he ever did.

Joe huddled in the corner confused. He didn't know what he should do to help. Joe kept replaying the last thing Ryan had said to him before going for the bat. Why did his brother botch their mantra? Dad must have told them it a thousand times.

Mrs. Yorp was preoccupied with Luke, Father Bob, and Samantha, while they continued to battle her vile soldiers. She didn't notice Grandpa and Ryan closing in on the mirrors from the other side of the room. Joe watched transfixed on their every move.

Grandpa loaded the bat behind his shoulder and swung as hard as he could for the middle of the first relic. Before he could feel the impact of his mighty hack, the bat ricocheted off the mirror and snapped back without so much as making a dent. Ryan stepped in front of him and grabbed the bat.

"What are you doing, Ryan?" Grandpa's eyes widened with surprise.

"Time to go see your son, old man," Ryan sneered. He twisted the bat and pivoted launching Grandpa into the mirror.

"No!" screamed Joe in horror. Ryan locked eyes with his brother. His evil, crooked smile was back. Suddenly, a tremendous explosion filled the room and threw Joe back into the wall. He looked up in time to see Luke, Samantha, and Father Bob being launched backward as well. Ryan, Haman, Herod, Delilah, and the snakes all seemed to vanish before Joe's eyes. He glanced toward the middle of the room. The mirrors were gone now, but Mrs. Yorp still remained.

"Ha-ha-ha, that is three now. You're the only one left, Joe. I can't be stopped. Don't try, or I will destroy you all. My kingdom awaits my return…" she bellowed as she slowly vanished before their eyes.

Luke helped Samantha up, and Father Bob checked

on Joe. Father Bob's face oozed with disappointment. They dusted themselves off and retreated to the elevator.

"What were you doing there?" Luke questioned Joe.

"Ryan thought you guys needed help, so we came up," Joe explained.

"He set you up. He came up here to help her." Luke spit out the painful truth disgustedly.

"Easy, Luke, he couldn't have known Ryan was going to do that. He's lost a lot today." Father Bob cautioned Luke.

"How did this happen, Father? What happened to my brother? I didn't notice anything different about him this whole time. Dad, Ryan, and Grandpa are all gone," Joe appeared crestfallen.

Father Bob was at a loss, "I'm not sure, Joe. He must have never been switched back in the attic, just like your dad."

"He was a plant to spy on us. She's been a step ahead of us this whole time. Yorp is toying with us. She knew exactly what we were going to do, and she led us right into her trap. Now they have Frank, and we don't know where she took the mirrors," Luke groused. The elevator doors finally opened up on the fourth floor. Already inside were Marissa, Ashley, and Breelyn. The girls could immediately read the looks on their weary faces.

"It didn't go well," Marissa whispered.

"What happened?" Ashley asked.

"They knew we were coming. It was a setup. We were lucky to get away. Mrs. Yorp and the mirror vanished," Luke muttered disgustedly.

"Yeah, I don't know where we go from here," Samantha agreed.

"Where are Grandpa and Ryan?" Breelyn asked.

"She has them." Samantha clenched her teeth.

No one said a word on the ride down, but they all were thinking the same thing. Where had Mrs. Yorp gone, and was she really unstoppable?

The elevator doors opened up on the bottom floor of the Office of Education. The Superintendent of Schools, Herm, greeted them there.

"How was your tour?" he said with a sinister smile. "I hope you were well taken care of."

"Fine," Father Bob replied tersely as they pushed past him and headed for the main door.

"Make sure you come back real soon. Ha-ha-ha-ha," Herm rubbed it in. "Say hi to Frank for me, if you see him."

Outside, they piled into the van with heavy hearts.

"What really bothers me is we had a chance to destroy that mirror two times. I threw a strike right into the middle of it as hard as I could, and Grandpa was going to smash it with the bat, too. Both times we couldn't even touch the mirror. I don't think it can be destroyed." Luke was beside himself.

Samantha nodded her head in agreement. Luke sat behind the wheel with his head bowed. "She told us we can't stop her, and if we try again, she will kill us all."

"What else did she say, Luke?" Ashley asked.

"That was it," he replied.

"No, then she said, 'my kingdom awaits my return,'" Father Bob corrected him.

"Right, meaning she's going back to that awful cave to torture all those souls some more and plan her next attack," Luke sighed hopelessly.

"No. That's not what Mrs. Yorp meant. I know where she is," Ashley offered.

Everyone perked up a little. "Where do you think she is?" Marissa asked.

"She's at Hill Valley Elementary. She's in her old classroom, Room 39," Ashley confidently answered.

"How could you possibly know that?" Luke asked dismissively.

"The day I was in her class, that's how she referred to her classroom. As 'my kingdom,'" Ashley remembered. "It always stuck with me because it was so odd."

"Maybe she's right," Samantha mumbled hopefully.

"I am right. Trust me," Ashley replied forcefully.

"Okay, let's say you are correct. That still doesn't solve our problem on how to destroy the mirror," Luke reminded them.

"We have to try though. If we work together, I think

we can do it. We have always gone after the mirror individually. Perhaps if multiple people are attacking it, we can get through her defenses," Father Bob surmised. "Fred wanted us all together for a reason."

"If we want to save Joe's family and stop Mrs. Yorp, we need to get to Hill Valley Elementary School," Ashley assured them.

11

HILL VALLEY ELEMENTARY

THE WEARY WARRIORS BEGAN THE 25-MILE drive to Mrs. Yorp's old school. Luke had taken over behind the wheel after Ryan's betrayal. Samantha sat up front with him. Marissa and Father Bob were in the middle seat, while Ashley, Breelyn, and Joe reclined in the very back row. The showdown at the County Office of Education had left them discouraged and distraught. Father Bob attempted to keep them from falling into despair. Joe's mind stayed busy brainstorming possible solutions instead of focusing on the loss of his family.

"Something isn't right," Joe whispered to Breelyn in the back of the van. "This isn't going to work. Why does the mirror keep moving? When I tried to destroy it, she protected that mirror. Now Luke tried, too, and the same thing happened to him. I don't think we can penetrate its defenses."

Breelyn and Ashley peered into Joe's eyes. Ashley heard the worry in his voice, but tried to reassure him. "I'm sure Father Bob knows what he is doing. Don't worry. We will get your family back. Father Bob believes if we destroy the mirror, it should release all the people trapped inside."

Joe shook his head. "I'm worried. I have a bad feeling." Suddenly a gust of wind in the van blew through the backseat. The Bible in Joe's lap flipped pages and rested open near the back. Joe looked up at the heading to see that it was Romans 5. Before Breelyn, Ashley, and Joe's stunned eyes, a passage slowly became highlighted in yellow. The verses were Romans 5:12 and Romans 5:18. They read the verses silently.

"Therefore, just as through one person sin entered the world, and through sin, death, and thus death came to all, inasmuch all sinned," read the first one. "In conclusion, just as through one transgression condemnation came upon all, so through one righteous act acquittal and life came to all."

"What does it mean?" Breelyn whispered.

"I don't know," Ashley answered.

"Maybe we should show Father Bob," Joe suggested.

Ashley nodded. "Father, we have something we need to tell you." Father Bob turned to face the back seat.

"What is it, Ashley?" Father Bob asked.

"Joe thinks we are making a mistake. We've tried to destroy the mirror three times, and have failed every single time." Ashley reminded Father Bob of what he knew all too well.

"I know, but this time we are going to attack it together and overwhelm Mrs. Yorp," Father Bob assured him.

"It's not going to work Father." Joe's conviction surprised Father Bob. The 8-year-old had been correct about a spy being amongst them. It was worth hearing him out on this matter.

"Why do you think that?"

"Dad's Bible flipped pages on its own and stopped here. Somehow these verses highlighted themselves before our eyes. We think it's a message to warn us about our plan. We just don't know what it means. Do you think you can interpret it?" Joe handed the Bible to Father Bob. He read the highlighted passage, and a pensive expression washed over his face. They waited in silence as Father Bob pondered its significance.

At long last, he spoke, "You say the verses weren't highlighted when it opened?"

"Yes, and then they slowly became highlighted as if someone were using a yellow marker to trace over them," Breelyn explained.

"What do you think is the message?" Joe asked.

"Well, the verses refer to sin and death entering into the world through Adam and Eve's disobedience to God. When Mary said yes to God, and Jesus sacrificed himself, death was overcome," Father Bob explained.

"Okay, but what does it mean for us?" Joe asked.

"Maybe a parallel is being drawn – an analogy of sorts," Father Bob hypothesized. "Perhaps through Mrs. Yorp's actions, death and evil entered into all of our lives. We would need to defeat the evil done by her with great sacrifice."

"Okay, but how do we do that?" Joe asked.

"And who is supposed to do that?" Ashley wondered.

"Well, we certainly have made sacrifices. Perhaps we all have to work together to destroy the mirror as we talked about. That will reverse Mrs. Yorp's evil and send her back to whatever cave she…" Father Bob began. He was interrupted by the Bible in his hand flipping to the last chapter, Revelations. Folded up inside the beginning of the chapter was a weathered piece of paper. Carefully, Father Bob unfolded the piece of paper. Written in black ink was a message, and Father Bob began to read. "I advise you not to focus on the mirror. To defeat this evil, you must use the book."

"What book is the note talking about? Does it mean the Bible?" Breelyn asked.

"I don't think so. It sounds like a different book,"

Father Bob surmised. "I'm sure it would have said Bible if that's what it meant. What book is it referring to, though?"

"I'm scared, Father. I feel like I'm never going to see Dad, Ryan, or Grandpa again," Joe blurted out. His eyes were watering. Father Bob's heart was moved with pity.

"You know, Joe, my father died when I was 7. He wasn't really there for me when he was alive, and then all of a sudden he was gone. I was crushed. For a long time, it tainted the way I looked at anyone's father. Even when I became a priest, the scars from my relationship with my dad made me doubt God's love for me. It was something I was still struggling with when we went to Grandpa's attic. I saw what Rick did for you guys, and it changed everything. Your dad showed what real fatherly love is all about – self-sacrifice. We will get him back." The determination and confidence in Father Bob's voice comforted Joe.

"I'm sorry Father, I have a problem with your God," chimed in Marissa. "How can a loving God allow all of these terrible things to happen to good people? How can he let Joe's family be trapped? How could he let my sister and all those other children be killed by Mrs. Yorp? I stopped believing in Him after that – my whole family did." Breelyn hung her head in shame. Her mother embarrassed her by challenging Father Bob.

Father Bob looked compassionately on Marissa. "I

can't imagine the hurt you have had to deal with in your life. I understand the feeling of doubting God and being angry. What you are describing is known as the problem of evil. Why would a loving, all-powerful God allow bad things to happen? He gave us all free will. Unfortunately, with that, some people choose to do evil. If he forced everyone to do good, then we would cease to have free will. In some ways, it is similar to being a parent. You want to protect your child from anything happening to them, any bad choices, or bad consequences. However, they will never learn anything, grow, or become their own person if you choose everything for them. He is the ultimate loving father. He tries to show us the way. God hopes we choose the correct decisions, but He allows us our free choices. No matter what, like a good parent, God is always there to help us. He loves us, and is always willing to forgive us. Tragically, some people's evil choices have dire consequences for others. However, God often can bring good out of great tragedy. Romans 8:28 says 'We know that all things work for good for those who love God.' Sometimes we just can't see the reasons in this life."

Marissa still looked a little doubtful. "I don't see what good could come out of all those children dying," she mumbled. Father Bob patted her on the shoulder and silently prayed for her. He continued to contemplate what the note in the Bible meant. He wondered if Rick or Fred were sending them messages to guide them.

"Joe found a note in his dad's Bible. We think it is a clue for us, but I can't figure it out. Does this mean anything to any of you?" Father Bob proceeded to read the note out loud to everyone in the van. They all shook their heads despondently.

"I have no idea what that could mean, other than breaking the mirror won't work," Luke replied.

"Wait a second," Breelyn said, pulling out something from her bag. "I just remembered I have this. I began reading this strange book right before Chloe and the mirror showed up." She held up her prized possession.

"I remember that book. I read it before," Ashley recalled. I think I was in third grade. The same time I met Mrs. Yorp.

"Oh yeah, that is a spooky book. I got it for my birthday one year. I think it was when you came and lived with us, Brandon," Samantha agreed.

Luke barely looked at the book. "Nah, I don't read," he replied dismissively.

"Are you sure, moron? Look again." Samantha chided him.

Luke enjoyed her verbal jousting so he inspected the novel closer. "It looks vaguely familiar. I may have read that when I was a kid."

"We found that book in the attic with the mirror. It was all ruined and damaged though," Joe exclaimed when he saw the book.

"What are the odds we all read this random book? It has to be the one referenced in the note," Samantha concluded. "It always coincided with strange or wicked things happening to us."

"Okay, so we destroy the book," Luke said. He grabbed the book and hopped out of the car.

"I don't know, Luke. We need to think this through," Father Bob warned. Luke ignored him and pulled a box of matches from his pocket. He put the book down on the side of the road and lit a match. Shielding the fire with one hand, he brought it closer to the book. When it was within a few inches of the book, the stick suddenly blew out. Luke lit another and tried again.

"Ouch!" he yelped and shook his hand. "It exploded in my fingers."

"Let me see the book," Father Bob called out. He took the book in his hand and ripped a page in half. The group watched in horror as the book seemed to repair itself right before their very eyes. The page fused together and was as good as new in a matter of seconds. "I don't think we can destroy this book either," Father Bob frowned.

"Great. What do we do then? Why would the note tell us about this book? There must be something we can do." Samantha thought out loud.

"I might have an answer for you in a minute," Joe called out as the Bible started flipping pages in his hand again. Tucked into the back cover, Joe discovered another note. He handed it to Ashley.

"That book does not belong in this world," she began reading. "As long as it is here, it will open up the possibility of destruction and allow Mrs. Yorp to execute her evil plans. Send it back through the mirror to close the portal, and free them."

"Of course. Both of them are indestructible, but if you join them, they may cancel each other out," Father Bob said. "Let's get to the school and stop her once and for all." They all climbed back into the van and started to drive the final two miles to Ashley and Grandpa's old school.

"I think we need everyone in there this time. You can bet Mrs. Yorp will have all of her friends with her, and we will need all the help we can get," Breelyn reasoned. "We need our whole team to work together."

"It's too dangerous, honey," Marissa explained. "You children can't go in there. Ashley can watch you in the van."

"Right. You guys stay in the van. We'll take care of Yorp this time," Father Bob agreed.

Breelyn looked down disappointed. "That's a mistake," she whispered to herself as Luke parked the van.

"Don't worry, they will be all right," Ashley reassured Breelyn while the four adults headed up the stone steps to the front gate of the school. They were disappointed to find the door locked.

"No one happens to have keys, do they?" Father Bob chuckled.

"Don't tell Breelyn that I know how to do this," Marissa pleaded. She removed a hairpin from her hair. In less than a minute, she had the lock picked, and they were inside the main school building.

"Okay, it's Room 39, right?" Luke asked.

"Yes, it is," an unfamiliar voice replied. Luke looked to his left and saw the county superintendent of schools, Herm. He stepped into the main entranceway.

"You people won't stop. It's pathetic. We are stronger than ever before. You will never stop…" Herm was interrupted by a fist crashing off his jaw. He dropped like a sack of garbage.

"I didn't like that scumbag, anyway," Luke muttered as he rubbed his fist. Samantha's mouth dropped open in surprise.

"Let's get going." Father Bob hurried the group along. They began the long walk up the three flights of stairs in a single file. Father Bob led the way, Samantha and Marissa followed closely behind, and Luke brought up the rear. He occasionally glanced back to make sure there would be no ambush from behind. In no time, they reached the third floor and made their way to the first classroom on the left. Father Bob checked inside his coat to be sure that he still possessed the book Breelyn had given to him.

"Okay, when we get inside, look alive. We don't know what Mrs. Yorp is going to have prepared for us this time. We have to assume she expects us because she has been a step ahead. If you buy me some time, I will get this book into the mirror. Remember, don't look into it directly." They all nodded at Father Bob's warning.

Luke turned the handle on the door and stepped inside, taking his position on the right side of the door. Samantha and Marissa followed him inside. Father Bob crouched down behind them. He hoped the element of surprise would allow him to get close enough to the mirror to fling the book into it. The room was pitch-black. Luke and Samantha ran their hands along the wall and found a light switch. Luke flicked it up and down, but to no avail.

"Come to try your luck again, priest?" The familiar evil voice broke the silence. "I warned you. Now I will have to destroy you all."

"I have a bad feeling about this," said Joe, channeling Han Solo in the van.

"I agree. We should have all gone up there. Fred brought us together for a reason." Breelyn tried to convince Ashley that they should follow the adults upstairs.

"Father Bob knows what he is doing," Ashley replied. "Let's give them a little more time." She longed to go up and help, too, but felt a responsibility to protect the children. Five more minutes passed, and their impatience grew.

"Father Bob is just trying to protect us, but if we don't help them, then we are going to be in danger anyway," Joe reasoned. "If we go now, we might be able to make a difference."

"Okay, but you two stay behind me and keep close. If I give you the word, you run as fast as you can to the police station that we saw down the street." Ashley made them promise. They climbed out of the van, and she locked the doors. Inconspicuously, they slipped into the front door of the school. It brought back childhood memories for Ashley. Everything seemed so much smaller now that she was an adult. They raced up the stairs, and Ashley's mind drifted back to her first day of third grade when she met the evil Mrs. Yorp. She never imagined that day would lead to this showdown all of these years later.

As they neared the third floor, evil laughter grew louder. Joe heard voices, but he couldn't make out what they were saying. Ashley thought she recognized pain in Father Bob's tone. Loud screams startled Breelyn, and she wondered if her mom was okay. They were only 10 steps away from reaching the landing area now.

"Ha-ha. I told you not to interfere with my plans. Your little family will not survive," Mrs. Yorp screeched in her raspy voice. Ashley peered discreetly into the classroom. She gasped at what she witnessed. Mrs. Yorp burst with laughter while Luke engaged in a losing struggle to Haman, Herod, and Ryan. They had driven him into the back wall next to the grandfather clock. Luke fought valiantly but was being overwhelmed. On the other side of the room, Delilah and two additional henchwomen pinned Marissa and Samantha into a corner. The former best friends attempted to fend off the evil creatures with crowbars, but they were ineffective. Mrs. Yorp called out instructions to her minions.

"Pummel them! Punish them! Bring them over here. They will make excellent additions to my cave!" she screeched. "Rick and Frank can't wait to see you all. He-he-he." Her raspy laughter irritated Ashley.

Father Bob waited for his opportune moment to make a break for the mirror with the book in hand. Ashley, Breelyn, and Joe slipped quietly into the classroom and crouched down behind a desk opposite Father Bob just in time to see him make his move.

Father Bob jumped up and deftly cut between two rows of desks. He stayed low so as not to be detected. He approached the glowing green mirror in the center of the room, and Ashley could hear him speaking. He was reciting the Latin phrases to activate and reverse the portal.

"If I can open it up, it may allow them to escape, and then I can throw the book inside to shut it down and destroy it," he told Luke entering the classroom.

Ashley watched as the mirror began to change colors from the green to white. Father Bob's recitation was working. When he closed to within 15 yards of the mirror, he reached inside his coat to grab the book. Unfortunately, the color change of her portal had alerted Mrs. Yorp. She whirled around in time to see Father Bob almost within range of throwing the book. He wanted to be sure his shot counted.

"No!" the evil, diminutive teacher screamed. Father Bob reached his arm back to fling the book toward the mirror. His arm never catapulted forward. Hal Goit appeared out of nowhere and lunged a massive paw toward Father Bob. He made contact with Father Bob's right elbow preventing his arm from exploding forward. The book slipped from his grasp like a quarterback being strip-sacked by a huge defensive end. It tumbled to the ground and slid 20 yards away from the mirror. Hal Goit enveloped Father Bob in a huge bear hug. The priest struggled to escape and recover the book with all his might, but it was no use. Hal's grasp was too tight.

"You failed again, priest," Mrs. Yorp yapped at him. "When will you learn? You can't win. Bring them all here," she ordered her cohorts.

"Gladly, your highness," Ryan sneered as they complied. The thugs brought Luke, Samantha, and Marissa next to Father Bob directly in front of the mirror.

"Why are you doing this, Heather?" Father Bob pleaded with her, stalling for time.

"Isn't it obvious? It's always been about family. Destroy someone's family, and you throw them into chaos. Destroy everyone's family, and the whole world becomes chaos." Mrs. Yorp savored her victory. While she spoke, Joe retrieved the book. He handed it off to Ashley behind the desk.

"Our master can thrive when there is maximum chaos," Mrs. Yorp continued. "Look at what I did to all of you. I took away your parents, your siblings, people you loved. Look at your lives – chaos. Now I'm going to take you away from the rest of your families and cause chaos in their lives. It's a domino effect, and with you out of the way, we will be free to continue our work. Total victory is only a matter of time, and you all will have a front row seat in my cave of despair."

"No!" Breelyn screamed. She couldn't bear the thought of her mother being taken from her. Mrs. Yorp and her horde of monsters whirled around and spotted Breelyn.

"More party crashers," Mrs. Yorp gurgled. "Let's make her feel welcome." She pulled out a stick and threw it down on the ground in Breelyn's direction. Instantly, the rod turned into a snake and slithered toward Breelyn. She put on her best soccer move, feigning going left with a quick hesitation and then exploding to the right.

It worked as well as it did on the field, and she breezed past the snake.

Meanwhile, Ashley had drifted near the middle of the room, about 10 feet away from Joe.

Mrs. Yorp raised her right hand. On cue, a wall of fire ignited forming a barrier around the mirror. The sinister snake recovered and continued its pursuit of Breelyn. Out of the corner of her eye, Mrs. Yorp spotted Ashley, who had circled around and plotted a diagonal course for the portal with the book in her hand.

"Well look at what we have here. It's the daughter of the one that got away. How nice of you to save me the trouble of hunting you down. Now I can ruin your mother's life like I was supposed to long ago." Mrs. Yorp flung another stick toward Ashley. This time her toss was perfect. The snake wrapped around Ashley's wrists and bound her hands behind her back. Once again, the book tumbled to the ground, but this time it fell at Ashley's feet.

"Breelyn!" Ashley's voice caught Breelyn's attention, and she recognized immediately what she needed to do. Breelyn adjusted her course toward the wall of fire. Ashley swung her right foot forward making solid contact with the book. It slid on a perfect course toward Breelyn. She cut in between the wall of fire and Mrs. Yorp's henchmen. The rogue snake grabbed Breelyn's wrist, throwing her slightly off balance milliseconds before Ashley's pass arrived. Ryan began running for Breelyn in an attempt to assist the snake. Breelyn steadied herself and concentrated on the pass. Her left foot launched forward, and felt her favorite feeling in the world. She had struck it squarely, and the book changed direction. It sped directly for Mrs. Yorp's mirror. Hal Goit dropped Father Bob and tried to block the book, but it was out of his reach.

No! You little brat!" Mrs. Yorp screeched. It was too late. Breelyn saw the book disappear into the mirror. A giant flash of light filled the room, and she threw her hands in front of her face to shield her eyes. She felt herself being lifted off the ground and dashed toward the classroom door. A tremendous blast launched everyone backward. The snakes instantly transformed back into sticks, freeing Ashley and Breelyn. The soccer stars could feel a cyclone-like wind sucking into the mirror. Ashley peered up in time to see Delilah, Haman, Herod, Hal, and imposter Ryan pulled back into the vortex.

"What have you done?! You can't stop us! This isn't over yet!" Mrs. Yorp screamed as she was slowly pulled toward her mirror. "Family will never survive. It will never surv…" And then she vanished. The mirror stopped glowing white. The room was silent, and the fire had dissipated. Luke and Father Bob got to their feet. Samantha and Marissa came over to check on Ashley, Breelyn, and Joe.

"I thought we told you to stay in the van." Samantha

stared seriously at the three of them. "I'm thankful you didn't listen." She broke into a smile and patted them on the back. They turned around in time to see Luke pick up the Louisville Slugger Father Bob had given him before entering the building. He strolled up to the mirrors in the middle of the room. He waggled the bat behind his right shoulder like he used to do.

"Batter up," he thought to himself as he put a picture-perfect swing into the middle of the first mirror shattering it into a million pieces. He handed the bat to Father Bob who did the honors with the second mirror.

"It's over. It's finally over," Ashley exclaimed.

"Where are Dad, Grandpa, and Ryan?" Joe asked as tears began to fill his eyes. Father Bob's face dropped as he realized they hadn't been able to rescue Joe's family.

"We're right here," Joe whirled around to see Frank, Rick, and Ryan standing in the doorway of the classroom. "As soon as you sent that book through the mirror and then smashed it, all of us were released." Grandpa turned to Ashley, Marissa, and Luke. "Captain Richard, Caitlin, and all of your mom's friends are at peace." Joe and Ryan embraced their dad and grandpa.

"Wait a second, how do we know they aren't imposters again?" Luke interrupted the family reunion.

"What's our motto?" Joe asked.

"If you boys stick together," Rick began.

"Work hard and help each other," Frank continued.

"We can do anything we put our minds to," Ryan finished the familiar mantra.

"It's them!" Joe broke into a huge grin.

"Come on, everyone. Let's get out of here," Grandpa exclaimed. Just like the students of the fire, he could finally be at peace. Father Bob's warriors helped each other down the three flights of stairs and out to Grandpa's van.

12

ONE YEAR LATER

FATHER BOB SIPPED FROM HIS MORNING cup of coffee. It was 10:30 on a Friday, and he was working on his second cup. The brew was a helpful companion while he put the finishing touches on his homily. He planned to preach on the holy family, God's desire for families, and the importance of it in today's society. Carefully he put pen to paper. Father Bob enjoyed handwriting his homilies each week. It made them feel more personal rather than typing them out on a computer. "Sister Lucia, whom Mary appeared to at Fatima in 1917, wrote that the final battle between God and Satan would be over marriage and the family." Father Bob attempted to drive home the point of just how critical good marriages and families are to God.

The doorbell rang, interrupting his train of thought. Father Bob sipped one more time and pushed up from his dining room table. He walked to the door and peered through the hole. He recognized the men standing outside and unlocked the door.

"Good morning, Frank. Good morning, Rick. Hello, Ryan. Hello, Joe." Father Bob greeted them warmly. "Great to see you. Won't you come in?"

"Good morning, Father. Sure, we would love to visit for a little while," Rick replied. They stepped inside Father Bob's humble residence and strolled into his living area. Father Bob sat in a chair while the other four plopped down on his couch.

"So what do I owe this pleasure today?" Father Bob asked cheerily.

"Well, Father, we wanted to talk to you about the men's group we are starting. We would like to use the hall to meet on Saturday mornings, if that is okay with you," Rick replied.

"Of course, I think this is a wonderful idea, and I want to do whatever I can to support you. What is your idea for the group?"

"We want to focus on what it means to live a Christlike life as a man. Somewhere along the way we have lost that in society, and we hope to try to bring that back a little bit," Frank explained. "We want to help each other be better fathers, grandfathers, sons, brothers, and husbands for our families."

"Excellent, excellent, that fits right in with this week's message." Father Bob's eyes lit up. "I'm going to work in Sister Lucia's prediction about the final battle." Frank and Rick nodded their heads.

"Do you think we saw the beginning of that last year?" Ryan asked him.

"Only God knows, Ryan, but I'm certain Yorp believed she was fighting that battle. I just want to help people see that we are in a war. We have to be aware of what the enemy is doing."

"Why did she want to destroy families?" Joe wondered.

"I don't know, son. Some people just lose themselves to evil little by little," Father Bob replied.

"I found some old papers while cleaning out the attic the other day," Grandpa began. "They were job reviews I took home from Hill Valley after that tragedy. I needed answers to help me deal with the pain and guilt. I wanted to know how, or why, someone could be so evil and hurt children. How could we not see it coming? I looked up all her job reviews since she started teaching at the school." His voice trailed off and he gazed out the window.

"Did you find anything?" Rick asked.

"You could almost see her transform through the reviews. The first five years, Mrs. Yorp received impeccable evaluations. Her principals raved about her teaching abilities. She had dynamic energy and made connections with the kids. She provided creative activities and had excellent classroom discipline. I remember talking to teachers and parents who had been around at that period. They claimed she was the sweetest person and everyone's favorite teacher. That's not the Mrs. Yorp I knew. When I continued looking at the evaluations for years going forward, the contrasts leaped off the page. She began getting mediocre evaluations. They would cite strange lesson plans and a lack of empathy for the students. What happened to her? I never figured it out. I'm just so relieved we stopped her, and those students are finally at peace."

Ryan patted his Grandpa on the hand. "So have you heard from the others?" Rick asked Father Bob.

"As a matter of fact, I just got this in the mail." Father Bob pulled a postcard off his coffee table. It had a picture of Samantha and Luke, and a handwritten note addressed to Father Bob. "They are doing well. They'll be back from the honeymoon next week, and said they would see me at Mass. Marissa and Breelyn have been attending our 9:00 a.m. service too. They are thinking of joining our RCIA program. Breelyn is having a great year in soccer, and her mom is more joyful than I have ever seen her. Ashley just called me last week to get some advice on the women's group she started on her college campus. I am so proud of all of you, and it gives me so much hope. Truly, so much good came out of all of us getting together."

"That's excellent, Father. We should get together with everyone sometime next week. Sunday is the first anniversary, it would be great to see everyone," Grandpa smiled.

"I agree. Let's do lunch after Mass. I'll let everyone know. We can…" A knock at the door interrupted Father Bob mid-sentence. "Excuse me for a second." He got up to answer the door. He returned a minute later. "A delivery," he informed them as he placed a package on the coffee table.

"Well, thank you, Father. We will let you get back to your work now. Tell everyone we are looking forward to seeing them next Sunday," Rick said as he stood up to leave.

"Okay. Thank you for coming over to visit. I will be at the hall Saturday morning to open it up for you." Father Bob escorted them out. After he closed the door, he returned to his homily on the dining room table. He began writing the next sentence, when he suddenly remembered the package on his coffee table. It was a small box, eight inches by 10 inches by four inches.

"Probably a copy of my book, 'Faith of our Fathers,'"

he thought. Parishioners were always sending him copies to sign. The fact someone actually wanted his autograph humbled Father Bob.

Quickly, he cut the packing tape using a kitchen knife. He pulled back the cardboard lid to reveal the book. Absent-mindedly, Father Bob opened it to the first page to sign it as usual, when suddenly something caught his eye. He didn't recognize the sentences on the first page. Father Bob began reading:

WARNING

Readers of this book BEWARE! You may think these are stories, but are they true? Tread with care, lest they happen to you. Ye be warned. Proceed at your own risk.

He knew he had seen this warning before. He closed the book so he could look at the cover. Father Bob's jaw dropped as did the pen from his hand. He recognized where he had seen this book before. It was the same book Breelyn had checked out of the library. The same book everyone in their group had read at some point in their lives. The same book Breelyn had kicked through the mirror last year. Father Bob kept staring at the title in disbelief.

"BEYOND THE SHADOWS," he repeated the words over and over to himself. Chills ran down his spine, and then he noticed a piece of folded up paper in the box underneath the book.

Father Bob unfolded the piece of paper and found a handwritten note. The edges of the paper were singed as if they had been burned. It appeared the message had been written by a shaky hand, but Father Bob could easily read the five-word sentence. "The War is just beginning."

Hobbling down the street away from the church and heading toward the elementary school was a tiny old lady. She had her hair pulled up into a bun, spectacles on her face and a walking stick in her hand. "Enjoy the book, priest," she muttered to herself. "He-he-he," her cackling, eerie laughter unnerved everyone she passed on the road.

You did not heed the warning. Now, strange occurrences await. If a sinister, short, old lady crosses your path, beware! You may have inadvertently traveled **Beyond the Shadows.**

www.ingramcontent.com/pod-product-compliance
Lightning Source LLC
Chambersburg PA
CBHW061615100726
47898CB00002B/678